AF204210

© 2021 Rolf Van der Wind

Verlag und Druck: tredition GmbH,
Halenreie 40-44, 22359 Hamburg

ISBN
Paperback: 978-3-347-32172-4
Hardcover: 978-3-347-32173-1
e-Book: 978-3-347-32174-8

The illusion of
forever.

Chapter I

Looking back.

We make some decisions, almost unconsciously. After so many years, I found myself walking along the long white beach, visiting a well-known spot that meant so much to her and me a long time ago. I thought of her and how she loved this part of the country. The sea's cold and sparkling blue seems to bring back yesterdays. Although I am aware that we will pass through death and ages lengthen before witnessing this scene together again, I feel close to Carol. Some memories are lasting. They are unique, and the details are the reasons for refusing to leave me alone. Today I drove close by without realizing where I was. Suddenly her memory crossed my mind, and it was then I decided to stop and revive old remembrances.

What we remember softens over time. What I remember is just that we were happy, not the individual moments that caused our joy. It was a different me when I was with her. She ignited the desire to change in me, to be a better person. So many recollections I would recast.

Carol's memories were tangible and heavy, and I had carried them with me long after we went separate ways. I have tried to block out the memories of the past. The memory of something painful retains its power. Every time they return, I get mixed feelings in my heart. Looking at pictures of those days is pleasant to me, which renews our time together and relieves the regret for their absence by a false and empty easiness and acceptance.

The existential error is to believe that the problem goes away by remembering the good times and forgetting the rest. Here on this white sand, Carol had laid down beside me and slid her arm beneath my head, lying her head on my chest. How much we did enjoy listening to the sound of the sea, reminding each other of the beautiful times and secrets we only knew. I can look back to the categorical knowledge that right then, at that moment, there was room for nothing but happiness in my heart.

She was a ray of sunshine, a lasting warm summer rain, a bright fire trying to stay alive inside my cold heart, and now she would not write or call me because she finally understood. She had tried with all her heart to save the man she loved but with time discovered that it was an impossible task. In the winter of our time, she realized that it was foolish to try to give something I did not want to have.

It feels sad and pleasing in this world of memories, where nothing is unknown to recall thoughts of yesterday. Now that it is all over, I see the wasted time in our life together.

Now I look back at so many years spent sharing fighting tears. After having fought, I recall knowing that I was happy to end the relationship but never did. Why can we not let the past die?

I knew she did not want more silent tears, no more gazing across wasted years but saying goodbye was hurting us too. Carol needed the strength to be able to say goodbye. Some changes in our lives are not freely taken but forced by events out of control. A sudden change of job or the end of a renting contract triggers the necessary steps that bring other changes to follow.

Later after a few months, gradually, her memory slipped a little, as memories do. There is an unconscious healing process within the mind that mends up our broken hearts despite our desperate determination never to forget. I do not want her to miss me simply because I will not ever know about that. It does not affect me anymore what she says or does.

Memories are images in our brain; each one brings its sorrow or its smile. It is sad and blue to see how a stranger became part of me, and after time that part of me left, turning her into a stranger again. It shows that we were ultimately never as one as we pretended to be.

Every morning I am slowly growing accustomed to the fact that one side of the bed would always be empty. The worst moments are when, walking along the beach, I realize that I have forgotten the exact blue of her eyes or the way her hand felt while walking hand in hand as we always did.

I was never in love enough to stay in love, never needed to leave anything unchanged, but the self-destructing notion in my mind demanding that everything must die overpowered my desire to stay with her. It is the life that matters, the eternal and constant process of getting in touch with reality and death. A world that only knows changes, and now all I have is my memories. The rest is gone, not forgotten, but over. Lovers long for everlasting love. It is easy to imagine the lover's desires but very easy to fail in their commitment.

I feel saddest for those who once knew what wisdom was but lost or became numb to the wonder of existence. We all need skills to defend, keep our spirits, survive, and find happiness. How easily we get confused and lose our ways. How crazy is it to try to force life the way we expect it to be? To believe that we can only achieve happiness when we conquer dreams but do not take enough time to decide what to dream. Why so many of us felt their emotions floating away and did not care about losing them, I guess it is horrifying, not caring enough about the loss.

I taught myself to display indifference to all the actions and passions of this world. Detachment is not giving up things but accepting the fact and being consciously aware that nothing is permanent. The possessions themselves were not the problem of my unhappiness; my relationship with possessing love and maintaining it caused destruction in my life. Since I practice scarcity as if the things I cherish are already lost or broken, I feel better.

I hope Carol never has to think as much as I think about her and our time together. I hope that her life goes as it went before we met. I felt nostalgic for what never was. We had good times, but there is a regret of not being able to be someone else. The absurdity of all this is that I knew it would happen, and, even worse, I know it will happen again and again because I like to be this way.

To think that everything is predetermined is boring and puts us like pawns on a chess table. If you are probably one of these people, you can probably be happy; you cannot do much after all. On the other hand, if all depends on your free will, you can probably enjoy the ride too. As long as you accept the conditions, you can be living a satisfying existence. The problem is on the rest of us, the eternally rebels with or without a cause. We do not take anything for granted, and nothing is deserved. No God to held responsible for the surrounding chaos.

I try to rebel against destiny. The chaos of my love is proof of it. Do you know what distresses me the most about her? If I sit down and start to write about her, everything about us feels like an eternity ago. I must admit that I do not know and maybe never knew her well. How many memories can I describe? Where did all go? But this is it. She is gone, and most probably, we will never meet again. All the chaos of sharing our lives is over. I would like to know if, for her, there were an instant worth remembering?

I guess I must retake my plans for today, knowing that somehow, she left a mark in me that I cannot erase and not forget even if I wish to forget all.

Before leaving the white sand of this beach, I tell the wind that saw us together last time I was here that I love her in my very own way. Trying hard to forget her and knowing that I will never do.

How could I have believed that she would just fade out of my mind like autumn leaves? She was a knowledgeable girl with a strong mind, with a good sense of humor and irony in her jokes. She will continue to be hardworking, creative, passionate in all that she does. The desire to reach her dreams will not let them be dreams forever.

This girl slipped out of my dream in my life, ceased to exist, but in my memories keeps returning, calling my name. One day I will reverse time and go back to the house where we lived together; I will again walk the streets we used to walk hand in hand. I will see her hiding behind a tree, waiting for me to come and scare me or steal something from my grocery bag. All of this I will do just to feel her closer, just to feel the pain in thinking of what could have been but never was.

Chapter II

A new horizon.

I t was still early in the morning when I opened my eyes. I could tell from the light in my room that another hot day was coming. Outside, the sky was blue, with not a single cloud on the horizon. I like these few seconds between dreams and reality. There is a pleasure in my hesitant consciousness, waking up to a new day.

A long time ago, I decided to look for a job that could allow me to travel and change places frequently. For the last 5 years, I have been working at a large company based here in the US. as a marketing manager. In my position, I am responsible for managing the promotion and positioning of a brand of products and services that my company sells. I must create and balance a competitive business strategy with a creative vision.

On one side, this job is a curse because no one voluntarily chooses to always change address and coworkers. After 5 years, I have maybe only two or three people I can call friends. On the other hand, it is a dream come true because it makes me feel alive. Since young, I had the rarest desire always to be somewhere else.

Most of my time, I do work with art directors, product developers, sales executives, public relations managers, and other employees to create engaging marketing campaigns. It may not sound awe-inspiring, but people like me are responsible for increasing global sales in many ways. I must be aware of global market trends and develop products that meet demand worldwide.

The IGUM Corporation was incorporated in April 1991. Our business concept is simply expressed uniquely. It offers products in the United States, Canada, Europe, and throughout Latin America.

When I joined IGUM in 2014, we already had customers in more than 45 countries worldwide. Nevertheless, the international expansion plans were far from complete. My work concentrated initially on domestic products, but later I was assigned to countries outside the US. My duty was to determine which countries would require longer-term investments and which had the potential to offer us faster near-term growth. We developed a five-part framework that can help the company to create a more targeted expansion strategy.

Working in marketing is more than merely selling a product internationally. Preferably, it includes the whole process of planning, producing, placing, and promoting a company's products in a worldwide market. Large businesses often have offices in the foreign countries they market to, but with the expansion of the Internet, even small companies can reach customers worldwide.

To be less technical, people like me need to understand what the customer wants to buy and achieve that goal.

Today I was consciously enjoying the gift of life that has been given to me. Though the room was quiet, my spirit was excited. I could sense the change the day would bring before I was even fully awake. A couple of weeks ago, I was asked if I would be interested in taking over a

Scandinavia position. For me, it was a considerable challenge, one I was thrilled to take.

After many uncomfortably quiet and sullen mornings, I decided to always play music at the start of a good day. Not only did these songs help me get through those Monday blues, but the music in general also helped me start all of my mornings on the right side of the bed despite waiting for a long day at work. Later I prepared another coffee, and it was just another morning that made me realize that the most plain-speaking things are enough to be happy.

This new opening outside the US pulled me to the edge of madness. There were hope and fear. I instinctively knew that a stay abroad was a prerequisite for growth and evolution.

Waking up and going out into the world without knowing what each day holds, taking life as it comes, giving up any illusion of control that was the way I wanted to live.

Personally, I am not a great fan of meetings. It is a waste of time most of the time, so I nearly never attempt one or organize one unless I know what result I want out of it. Big companies tend to have too many meetings but no agenda, and by the end of the day, they have reached a resolution on absolutely nothing.

Today it was different. This meeting occurred at the precise moment in my career when I needed a change in my life. Now it was precisely when it would have the most significant impact on me.

In a startup, it does not matter if you are right all the time. What matters is having forward momentum and understandably presenting your vision.

At the end of the day, there were reasons to celebrate. I was the newly appointed manager of our office in Stockholm, and to my delight, the position was to be taken almost immediately.

I remember thinking to myself, "Sweden, I am coming. We may be complete strangers until will be not."

Many events added together in my mind until I felt that the time was ripe for looking back over the week, the year, and trying to figure out where I came from and where I was going to. This upcoming change was sincerely welcome. I felt that the time was right to start a new chapter in my life to change not only the address but myself. Personal growth was not planned to please others. I wanted to be different to emphasize interpersonal relationships. If the period living with Carol taught me something, that could be explained by saying that sharing life includes more than sharing a bed. When you start faking who you are, you start lying to yourself.

In the end, nobody has a chance to be happy.

Nobody must remain the way they are forever. We should be the person we aspire to be. Actual change requires work.

To think that only because I was going to be in a new country does not bring change automatically. I was convinced that the process would take time and effort. Rewarding personal growth requires motivation, the desire to educate yourself, and the willingness to make changes. I also needed to be prepared to get out of my comfort zone and sometimes do uncomfortable things, but I am convinced they are for my own good.

I have often heard people say, "Time heals all wounds." but I disagree. In time, our mind, protecting its sanity, find a way to lessen the pain, but it is never gone. I do not want to win Carol's heart back because deep inside, I know we would cry and hurt each other again. I still remember how strange I felt after she left. Even now, waking in the night, I miss not having her sleeping beside my side.

Sometimes listening to a song can take you back instantly to a moment bringing about beautiful things. The music will always remain the same tune, just like the memories. Undoubtedly, some things have to be forgotten if we want to go on living. The trouble is that beautiful moments exist not in what is seen and remembered but in what you keep in your heart, unable to forget. Carol used to joke about my easiness, forgetting the past. For me, it is sometimes primordial to forget or at least to try not to remember.

Fortunately, no matter how deep and unsatisfied I was feeling with myself, someone always watched over me. My father died years ago. I was very young and have not many memories of him. My mother was different; she was always there for me. The day she left this world, I was far away. It felt more comfortable to be so far away because I was exempted from grieving and saying the last farewell.

When one of our parents goes, then you know. Your life is ending. I know that well; her parting gave me a better understanding of myself. May her spirit allow me to manifest, create, and stop doing wrong. All her love will keep shining on me, helping me to reach beyond what I ever thought possible.

As an only child, I got accustomed to being by myself, and not having a large family made it worse. So, my mother and I spent a lot of time reading, listening to music or doing sport. I wanted a little brother or a little sister growing up, but I am happy I am an only child. When I hear all the trauma, some friends have dealt with brothers or sisters.

Maybe it was pathetic, but I wanted to live in a world where I could reproduce the stories I read in books, especially the romantic ones. I definitely gave myself more chances to put into practice all I had learned in the books than I should, but the end was never what I expected. In the heart matters, you cannot play a role and hope to experience true love.

By the time I was close to 30, my list of girls was numerous. When I seduced a girl, and she accepted, my body did go, but my heart stayed behind.

If Carol had not crossed my path, I would possibly be an irreparable case. She was who showed me the meaning of love. Now when I look into a girl's eyes, I care to know what the girl sees. If she is in search for love, I will not try to be a lover. I am in search of genuine love that reaches beyond the vague thrill of the conquest.

The desire to become a loving man shines through my mind and gives me the key to writing my history, not a copy of someone else's.

Life throws challenges, and every challenge has a learning curve; I do not expect to be Mr. right guy but a decent one. I would rather have my heart broken by girls that do not deserve me than breaking the hearts of girls who honestly loved me.

Chapter III

A new man.

The day I return to my home country will never be the same as if I had never left. Sweden has changed me in more ways than someone can imagine. It may have been a slight change initially, but with time turned to be a dramatic difference in my way of seeing the world. Some of my life approaches were so confusing that I don't even recognize myself today. Once my mindset changed, everything had a different meaning.

Tomorrow I will be celebrating one year since my arrival in Europe. Looking back, I see the person I used to be. For me, success was everything, and the effect on me was horrible. Gladly things are distinct, and I cease to be obsessed with the idea of success and money.

I cannot help fearing that I will be thinking the same way about my actual way of living in ten or twenty years. The strangeness of time. Not in its passing, in the irreversibility that comes with constant change. No matter how long we could exist, the change will always be part of living. I like myself better today, but that does not mean I am continuously developing into something better. The scary part is that people do not realize how much the world around you changes until we hit a point where we must either change or self-destruct.

Some things touch me in inexplicable ways. A song, a sentence, or a thought while driving around the streets bring me an inch away from weeping, and somehow, I feel ashamed of my sentimentality. It is most distressing to have a sentimental heart.

Remembering my casual relation with girls, I can feel when there is a distance between the girl and me. I can sense a girl feeling the usual alienation from me because I did not automatically love or see important matters the same way. Almost every girl I know has a very grounded idea of how her life is supposed to develop. In no way would I say that man does not have a vision of the future, but we are more open to take crazy risks just for some inexplicable reason. You can hang out with another stupid person like you who is ready to play Russian roulette, and I doubt that person will be a woman.

I never thought to be a good boyfriend. My conception of forever is vaguely close to an inevitable end. I understood a long time ago while Carol was with me that there was a flaw in my reasoning, just as there was a deficiency in my ability to love.

Something pinned to me once. The awareness that time cannot be stopped and that there is no going back or regaining a heart for a moment or doing things differently. Carol is often in my mind but unreachable in my current reality. Maybe I am a sentimentalist who wants to have the luxury of an emotion without doing what is necessary to earn it.

There is a girl somewhere I have never seen before. She will be the person of a dream I had a night thousand years ago. Until then, I could not avoid worshiping others who had little bits of her. This way, the waiting does not turn into intolerable suffering.

In my confused mind, I do not put great affection on objects. To sentimentalize items would be to put too much importance into something that is not there. I do not keep photographs or souvenirs no necessity to put emotions on objects. If something stirs in us unique feelings, I force myself instead to look only at its reality.

To be known as a cold and lonely person did not bother me much. At least that is what I told myself on lonely nights when sleep eluded me and my fears hunted my peace while the cold wind pierced my soul.

A slow grin spreads across my face. A girl called me once a lover with attention deficit disorder, and probably that was an accurate description of myself years ago. Today I would undoubtedly get better ratings but never top grades. My problem is that I believed one girl would come my way and nurse me back to health. Having so many roads in front of me, knowing which leads to her, is the hard part. It is relatively easy to find someone willing to spend time with me, not for exceptional reasons, just for the simple reason that my work depends on having social interactions. The worse way to impress a girl is by forcing the moment. You may think getting somewhere and then all at once it gets awkward. If something is not natural, let it go. Most of the time, it will get you not what you wish. I enjoy the hours between a boy and a girl are in an acquainted relationship and the moment after. It happens in a whisper. Something starts developing, taking the relationship to look at her as a girl and her looking at me as a boy. A soft touch of her skin, a coming closer, an in-depth look into each other eyes. Many little things change the future of both social butterflies forever.

I keep finding the ashes of the man I unequivocally used to be. How hard it is to change, I vaguely imagined. I continue to see myself smiling and saying, "Ok, fine!" but faking it every time. Although it is altogether abominable, faking your feelings is easier to a certain point. I aspired to identify myself as a romantic guy, but women saw me more as a refreshingly unsentimental one. That was confusing, and the best way to deal with this dilemma was to get as many opinions as possible. Of course, the more affairs I got involved in, the more discrepancies came to light. By the end, it was not unusual for me to be flirting with anything that would pay me any attention. It was more evident that if I were going to let people judge me, the verdict would always be different. These short love affairs would end commonly the same way. In my mind, there is no counting of the times a girl told me, clearly confused and disappointed, "I do not understand what you are doing."She was not the only one; I did not know either. The so-called game of love I played did not give me any victories. Maybe Carol was the last girl giving in to my ways, but she was the final warrior stabbing my knife deep in my heart, living me to die a slow and painful death.

The last days with Carol were not sweet as we would have wished. Even as the last words spoken between us were coming out of my mouth, I was enormously despising myself for saying them. At that time, my anger was controlling me, and the regrettable choice of words resulted from not knowing how to do right. Today I have nostalgia for what never was and dissatisfaction with my old self.

I promised to call a girl I do like and feel attracted to, but my new me is not ready yet. Old habits are hard to break. If all goes wrong and my intentions of becoming a better version of myself go down like raindrops into asphalt from where nothing grows, I would end drunk and jumping from any bridge high enough to send me to hell. Could it be that the time we spend trying to change is like chasing clouds?

If I wait too long, she most probably thinks that I am not interested in getting to know her or starting reasoning that I do not care. After spending a long troublesome time, recognizing that I had thrown away a girl's love only because I was pretty ignorant of its worth, I did not wish to fail with my next relationship. We do not have to be defined by our failures or things we did not do. I wanted to tell her everything, be honest, and listen to what she had to say. Was I insecure about feeling? It is realistic to believe that I refused to love something because I feared losing something I loved.

Not everything is perfect, especially at the beginning. Maybe one day, one can only hope not to regret our mistakes too much. Carol told me once that she had asked for someone to come into her life, but who came was never able to accept her offer of companionship for the time she intended. I will always be wondering what could have been. Yes, I am afraid to start. If only I could take this slowly and not rush things, then maybe all would be easier.

Chapter IV

Avery.

A ghost inhabiting the mind of a stranger is the best way of describing myself these days. I do not want to think about tomorrow. If I do, I will go crazy. If we wait for things to be perfect, we would probably wait eternally. After postponing my date with this girl from the office, I did call her yesterday, and she agreed to go out to dinner tomorrow night. Her name is Avery. She is a beautiful girl and a curious soul. One thing that struck me about her was her spontaneous interest in things that meant nothing to other people. Some quantifiable external beauty always attracts me, but Avery had that particular undefinable something that made her special. You rarely fall in love without being tempted to see, interestingly, the wrong values in the person. A few weeks ago, Avery was far from suspecting that she was becoming an object of interest in my eyes. We worked in different sections and occasionally met in meetings. I had looked at her without second thoughts, but after some days, I gazed at her only to find more and more pleasure in her presence. It took not long until I admitted that she was graceful and pleasing to have close. She projected positivity around her and became a sun in the center of my galaxy.

Matt, my best friend, could not explain the mysteries of her attraction to me, nor logic could explain it satisfactorily.

Later that afternoon, we went to a nearby coffee shop, and Matt was still jocking about my draw towards Avery. He said, "It is what you do not see you are interested in." It was like my old me talking to me. I knew that he meant it as a joke, but nothing touches you more than a reminder of what you are trying to avoid doing. Matt looked at me and said, "Oh yes, I know that look. What are you thinking?"

I smiled back and told him, "I accept the hard reality that I maybe might be imagining too much and that she is far from interested in me." Matt, in his peculiar way, asked, "Do you know what she sees in you now?" Before I could answer, he started laughing and said, "This is the guy I would follow to hell and back." I was not able to answer. Why does something that someone tells you scare you so much? Maybe deep inside, I always have an idea of love. Fantasy love is much better than reality love. The situation was curious. How does someone like Matt Peterson put me in doubt? Did he misjudge me? Do people get the wrong impression about what kind of person I am? Indeed, I am far from "The perfect guy." The most accurate definition of myself would be "Extremely confused and dangerous."

After leaving the coffee shop, Matt went home, and I decided to walk around to clear my mind. After all, it is not like tomorrow I would get married; it was just a first date, nothing more. If you always add positive emotions to the things you want, then the better your chances are. I tried to imagine how things would go.

I saw telling her, "It is you I think of when I wake each morning. It's your face I dream of." Again, I try to keep an open mind and hope to find fabulous things showing up in my life. I was too engaged in my thoughts that I did not hear someone asking me something. When I turned around, I saw two women strangely looking at me. I apologized for not realizing they talked to me and asked both ladies if I could help. The younger girl asked with a strong accent for directions. I thought to myself that most probably they spoke English because the accent is easy to recognize. I knew the street they were asking for and gave them directions in English. Both started laughing and were happy to have found another American.

Because the street they wanted was in my direction, I offered to walk together. While walking, I learned that it was mother and daughter going on a trip across Sweden as the family originated from here. This encounter was a completely unexpected turn of events that took me unaware and swept away all my thoughts. During walking, I wished that the street would be farther away from where we were. By then, I knew they were from Minnesota and probably would stay for another two weeks here. The rare moments that come unannounced are the most magical. When we arrived at the street where they lived, she gave me her phone number and made me promise that I would call her. I looked at her, unsure of how to answer. Finally, I promised her that I would do so and said goodbye. I left without looking back, somehow knowing that the crazy thing I just did was well-intended but not according to what I wanted to do. No one knew what was wrong with me or what kind of sick joke my head was playing. I was nice, but it was more than being nice, which was precisely the point of my disappointment. You cannot let all be a game of playing Mr. nice guy just for the pleasure of getting a phone number. Was I not thinking about my next date? Is it so easy to make me go for any chance of chasing a girl? The fact of letting things roll bothers me. I should have clarified my actual intentions and not left room for welcoming ideas. My first nature hides but never goes away. Sometimes, it feels like I will stop breathing when I force myself to the new vision of my better self. I do not want to let go of my priorities, and even if the road gets bumpy, I must stay my course.

Tomorrow will be a new day and will bring a new set of opportunities. All I can do is stay committed to myself and persist in trying to be a better person. What lies inside me is more significant than what lies ahead of me. Today I am more conscious of life. For me, it means we have the chance to transform into what we wish to be. Learning from our mistakes inspires us to create a life we love. It may be a dangerous undertaking when you fight yourself to discover the real you. I am not fighting evil; I do not expect to transform darkness into light, only to be more content with dealing with other human beings.

I want things to go well tomorrow. I've been alone for a couple of months, and now I am ready to have a relationship. Why should I have high expectations? Better do everything for its own sake and see where all goes. Our mental expectations are probably a futile attempt to put permanence on something temporary. I am committed to treating Avery gently and truthfully; it is not what I expect from her but what I can offer her. Years ago, I would decide to take action in a new relationship as my needs and demands required avoiding other concerns. I now see that we cannot expect the outcome to meet our stipulations and goals if we only think of ourselves. It was downright depressing, and no girl could complete the list of demands without losing the essence of being herself. The girls who did intend to fill my list of expectations did so in a cancerous way to themselves. In the end, we had to terminate the relationship to survive.

Our sentimental life is a place where heaven and earth collide in a baffling clash of hopes, dreams, fears, and sometimes nobody survives. It is still fresh in my memory of the day Carol told me, "I have been trying to make you happy for a year now, hoping somehow that you would learn how to love me, but I do not think it is working." I see now that confusion is the only possible result of a one-person relationship, and I am about to change that.

Although my plans were unavoidable, the short encounter tonight was still on my mind. I could not decide to forget and turn off the noise in my head. Until I would not make the unconscious conscious, it would direct my decisions. Maybe the meeting's unexpected characteristics did not give me enough time to handle the situation the way I would have fancied. I needed to find a way to calm my thoughts. Unfortunately, I must face the mirror every day, and it is not my plan to avoid them forever. It took me not long to find an escape. The best would be to call and meet with Lucy and her mother. Why not invite them to lunch, letting me come out of this in a fair and friendly way. This solution brought convenient peace to my silly head. This feeling of peace was agreeable. I have begun to listen to the teaching my consciousness whispered to me. Now, I was not afraid to look in the mirror on the opposite next time when I will look at myself again, I will see that I am suddenly more open to change than I ever was before.

Trying to stay and follow my rational thinking is elemental for archiving my goals, but emotions make me human. Even the bothersome ones have a purpose. Trying to lock them down would make them louder and more dangerous. I should try to keep them on a leash, always present but under control.

It would be much more beneficial for myself and my plans if I learned to distinguish between valuable and worthless ways to deal with what life offers me. It is not the pursuit of pleasure that I have in mind. It is the amount of positive vibration that will radiate in life that matters to me now.

I do not want to be defined by what type of food I eat or where I live, or what car I drive. Identify me by the ends I am living for. I want to live for things given to me for a purpose. It does not matter what I did or where I was, but it matters where I am and what I will be doing. I think it is satisfying to live not knowing than to have answers which might be wrong. I am not sure of anything. There are things I do not know anything about, and about that, I am pretty convinced.

Tomorrow is going to be an exciting day. Our life is full of uncertain questions, but it is the endurance to seek answers that continue to give meaning to life and finally define who I am.

Chapter V

First date.

The morning started wonderfully quiet. I thought about Avery the moment I opened my eyes. Girl, I think you still have no idea about the effect you can have on me.

In my mind, I had the answers. I knew what I wanted that day. The amount of positive vibration was enough to fulfill my ego's desires and enter into the silence of my heart.

To believe that limitations are imaginary has always helped me achieve things that I would not even try otherwise. Preferentially it makes more sense to me to see the sparkle of a star than only the blackness of the night.

I seemed to have walked all day endlessly during work, awaiting the hours to be with her. I had chosen a small restaurant on the first floor in front of an empty marketplace for our date. This place was cozy and quiet; it had small tables in front of each window with a city view. It indeed had the perfect atmosphere for a romantic date.

The nearness of her was all I longed during the day. Could it be that when you desire someone, they are probably feeling the same? I do not think she can miss me as much as I am longing to see her tonight. It is weird to feel you miss someone you are not even sure you know.

Time does this, sometimes. It keeps you in a state where time seems to slow down, and hours do not go as fast as always. A clock measures time precisely. The estimation of time by the heart and the head is considerably different. Time can fly or stay still, depending on what is happening in your head or heart.

I was almost going to go when my phone rang. It was Avery; her voice was soft but resolute. She said that she was not coming.

Things that happened a long time used to seem way off, but now it was like yesterday was catching up. Expecting fervently for something and realizing that all was a construct of your mind, reality seems to be off. The common question is, "What did I do to make her not get involved with me." A silence surrounds my heart and fills it again with discouragement. Did I expect too much? The feelings that hurt most, the emotions that trouble us most, are those we have no control over. I do not know what they to call, the spaces between seconds, but I had to decide how to fill the emptiness of time she left, saying no. These changes were not going to let me find peace in my mind. I decided to go and eat at the restaurant I had selected. Staying home was only going to make me feel down. It was early enough for me to walk to the center where this little place was. The weather was very agreeable although I wished for rain. Many yellow leaves were on the ground, but autumn was not entirely here yet. I wanted my heart to stop bleeding. My thoughts were always returning to this girl. Life shows us all colors, some bright and gray shades, and now my world was closer to dark gray. My feet moved almost without the help of my brain. I turned left at the corner, and before me was Avery. It must have taken me an eternity to speak; finally, I only said, "Hi, this is very odd." She was as surprised as I. To my amazement, she said, "I was thinking of calling you; forgive me, I am a mess." After a bit of silence, she continued saying, "I wanted to apologize; it is all my fault and handed me her phone."

My number was on display, but she did not press the call button. With a sweet smile, she added, "What was I supposed to say?" By that time, I had figured it all out. Things went from gray to rose-colored rainbows. The past few seconds defined the rest of the day. I looked at her; she was gorgeous. Her blonde hair moved in waves in the wind, and those deep blue eyes were enchanting, leaving no place for any other feeling that attraction. I invited Avery again to our planned date to calm her down, telling her to forget about the initial phone call. She was happy to accept, and we laughed about the craziness of all. These are the split instants that make life memorable. What are the chances of meeting around a corner? Memories of this particular afternoon will never end, but life does one day.

While walking, I was tempted to grab her hand but decided to wait until the right moment. I had the feeling that she accepted my approaches positively but going slow is mostly the best strategy.

I like the memories that are burned in the back of our minds and make us remember. Undoubtedly this afternoon was going to be one belonging to that category.

I loved the way it felt being with her. She was not complicated at all. I must admit that the effort you may want to invest is never enough to keep a relationship. It must be something there that maintains all alive.

That soul who cupid made me fall for was an angel from the heavens; every minute went like seconds flashing by. I did not want the evening or the night to arrive. I wanted to stay there taking, watching her face, registering every expression on her face. I was able to see the part of her that only I was allowed to see. The attraction I felt for this girl was turning into dependency. I would not let her return to her world, or at least she would have to take me with her. I thought I achieved the meaning of life; never did I felt so exhilarated; I did not understand what was happening to me. Each hour passed as if it was my heart that allowed time to exist.

We talked about the most varying subjects from philosophy to a book I lost and was impossible to find during that evening. Avery told about earlier years and her family. We agree to visit them before the autumn ends. Avery said, smiling, "One day we will go so that I can introduce you to my parents and my two sisters, you will need to do things for me that you dislike, but that is what it involves to be part of a new family." I answered, "That sounds terrific, not to mention that your sisters must be gorgeous as you. Yeah, that sounds like a perfect family reunion". Surprisingly she laughed and said, "I love people who make me laugh, but I have bad news for you; you are only mine."

By the end of this dinner, I was not able to control my hands. I had to touch the girl, to feel the warmth of her skin on mine. I gently took her hand as she was gesturing something. It was a second when I said a thousand words without sound. She did not pull her hand back; I could feel her pressing mine in return. I looked at her eyes and said, "It has been a wonderful evening, better than I ever expected." thank you for changing your mind. I do not remember when or if I let her hand go again.

The magic of someone new hardly lasts long enough to impress me sufficiently, but Avery was uncommonly attractive. She possesses a deep understanding of human behavior. It is a shame that such talent is not recognized and exploited at work. It was as if she felt a deep positiveness of everything. Her curiosity did attract me in the office, but in the end, it created with other workers a sense of isolation since it divides more than it unites. It is hard to find people eager to learn even topics that are not appealing at first sight.

When we decided to leave the restaurant, it was late. I told Avery that we would share a taxi. We went first to her place. She got out of the car, and I went with her to the door of the house. We promised each other to go out again. Her face denoted happiness and sincere wishes to undertake something together also. My eyes slink over her, and I said, "I neglected to tell you- you look lovely." We wave good night, and I continue home.

The night was now cold, but inside me, a warmth that originated deep inside my heart kept me unaware of the outside temperature.

Often the fairest impression that remains in our minds is the closest to the truth of the person we spent time together. Tonight that sentence was a confirmation of a genuinely fantastic encounter.

At home, the uncommon desire to share this feeling invaded my soul. What was in her personality that attracted me so much? I knew she was good-looking, but it was not the outside looks that caused this attraction. It was something deeper, something that felt uniting me with her in a very unusual way.

Could I say that I was in love? Did I fall in love because we have looked at each other and so love started? It appears too simple but is that not the way love always finds his way to our hearts? Considering that I am not new in the heart matters, too many questions were escaping my reasoning. My old conceptions about passion spontaneously revived, but this time I was not after an affair; I was looking to start a long relationship. I wanted to fix myself a drink when the phone rang. On the other side of the line was Avery. She was first a little hesitant, but soon her voice was clear as always. I could hear her say. "Tonight was... well, it was perfect for a first date." "I was thinking of you this very moment," I told her and added, "You have turned my world upside down; that is the least I can say." The easy playfulness of her call was more than a clear sign of an inevitable long relationship coming our way.

Chapter VI

Less a stranger.

A year ago, Avery and I were not acquainted; we were complete strangers. Today she is the center of my world, the reason I smile in the morning. To think of being far from her as the stars in the sky separated by millions of miles is unbearable. Now, as we stand two feet apart and stare at each other, life feels so different. Until this moment, I had not understood that this was what I never appreciated before in my life. I had taken refuge in superfluous relationships until I became confused with my own reality. I used not to care about who I was living together with, which can be a huge mistake, for by doing that, I may have entertained angels without knowing it. Angels that will never return because there are no angels anymore.

I feel the guilt of having cut hearts out with no remorse. Yet each man kills the thing he loves. Sometimes to discover your love for someone, you must self-destruct love to appreciate what you lose.

Yes, I was in love once and killed love. I believed to know that I could imagine how much this would hurt, but I was wrong. Not physical pain hurts so much. You feel as though you will bleed to death with the pain of it. Something was telling me, "You better not die today. You might truly go to hell."

The worst part of retaining the memories is not the pain attached to them. It is the loneliness of it. I' have been depressed. I have felt awful, willing to die, and beyond all empty. The loneliest moment in my life was when I watched the whole world fall apart, and I knew it was my choice. Although there is much I owe to the hard times I went through; there is no wish to return to those dark places.

My final assessment was that all I ever wanted was to reach out and touch another human being, not just with my hands but with my heart.

Some wounds do not let marks on the body, injuries that are deeper and never truly heal. This new creation of myself was the hopeless attempt to escape from my old ways. I did not want more torturing memories. It was not satisfying to have the insupportable inability to ruin every relationship. That life was conducting me to some inescapable approaching doom I needed urgently to avoid.

Perhaps love is a minor delusion. The one person who can relieve us of the chains we have chosen to tie us with is our recipient and source of love.

What combinations of shadows and fears are still on the soul that holds me confused and threatens the future I so yearn for my future?

Avery, would it not be better if we keep this desire hidden inside our hearts and never actually got together? This way, love and dreams would always be inside us. That hope would be a small glimmer warming our hearts. It would be a tiny fire protecting us from the cold of being alone, a flame that the violent winds of reality might easily blow out.

People say that love does not fear. I think that the fear of losing your love fills me with extreme terrors never felt before. Now, I need to calm the beat of my heart. If one day I lose, the fear of losing your love will only show me that I do not love you right.

Love does make me strong. Strong to never give up on you. It does not matter in which dark place I wake up at night. I will stay there wondering, fearing, dreaming dreams no mortals ever dared to dream, but you will never walk out of my heart. You may one day not be by my side, but you will always live in my heart.

Could it be that I came to this world to be alone? I like and enjoy solitude. It is not darkness. To be in nature is never to be alone. Part of us needs other humans to understand the world. For me, I am not alone when walking for days through a forest. It is beautiful, it is endless, it is full of life everywhere, and yet if you do it for a long time, all seems empty. It satisfies a part of us and hurts another. If you do not enjoy being alone, then, of course, we can call that experience a dark and hollow space full of disappointment and loneliness. I like to believe when we can be alone, we can be with others without using them to escape loneliness.

Once a long time ago, I had a short relationship with a girl I tried very hard to help and understand. Her name was Tricia. She was cold in her way of expressing her feelings. I wanted to get closer, but it was impossible to read her mind. She may have told me that she was complicated and challenging, but I was not ready to believe that it could be true. In the end, I blame the lack of communication for a miserable kind of love relationship between two people willing to try love. Despite talking to each other, despite qualifying as intelligent and open to intuition and sympathy, we never really communicated anything to each other. The essential substance of our feelings remained incommunicable. That experience showed me how poor language is. How difficult it is to use words for expressing thoughts and feelings. In a way, we had a sentence to perpetual solitary confinement.

How can I have both? I want to love Avery the best way I can, and I like the ecstasies of seclusion. The worst kind of loneliness in the world is the isolation I experienced with Tricia. The solitude that comes from being misunderstood; it can make us unwillingly lose grasp on reality. Thinking of how I lost my composure brought me to look in a mirror, wondering how ugly a person could get and how all was supposed to be in the name of love. I remember the frustration of feeling not getting what I longed for despite my efforts. Frustration resulted from not being able to know if she was authentic in her feelings.

I thought it was not essential to get signs of love, tenderness, attraction, but Tricia's ways were cold, and I did suffer emotionally with it but never intended to confront her about this. In a way, I wanted to accept her the way she was but did not manage to do so. In a relationship, you must adapt to your partner. You do not stop loving someone just because they are unable to express their feelings. I do not think so. That is what makes the failure in our communication hurt so much. It slowly brings pain, frustration, anger, and worse of all, I still loved her. I still think I do. Now I do not like to think about her; it only brings misery. I will tear my lips out if they mention her name once more. I want to take all her memories about me away and hope she will never see me again. That was the strangest kind of love I ever experienced. In no moment was hatred present; it was only frustration and sadness of something good that went wrong.

I learned from that experience. When I look back and think of Tricia, it is primarily disappointment I left behind. I know deep inside there is a part of me that can do horrible things. Consciously I always try to do good, never trying to hurt anyone, yet good intentions are never enough. I could become completely self-centered, even cruel. There is no surprise to see the road to hell paved with good intentions.

Time helps me to see some aspects of the past differently or from another point of view. Regrets are part of making decisions that is unavoidable, and I will carry the scars of many bad choices. With Tricia, my heart ended full of wounds and almost no memories to slow down the bleeding. I remember looking at a picture of her someone took of her by surprise. I like that picture very much; something about the sadness in her face is fascinating to me. The last time we spoke, she told me, "Do not worry, I will retire to my corner and get strong again." It is sad for me to see a girl that used to have a heart feeling safe in a corner all by herself. My greatest regret is failing to take her out from a place she does not deserve to choose as home.

Like in every relationship with Tricia, we had some good moments I do not throw away to the ashes of burned memories. The sweetest memory is one after an argument. I got out of the car and wanted to go away. After crossing the street, she got out of the vehicle, calling me, "Do not go away." I knew how hard it was for her to do that. It was one of the few times she demonstrated to care. For a moment, her face was open and vulnerable. I caught my breath, and with tears wanting to rush out of my eyes and heart, turned back and got into the car. Tricia was a girl that could have had me if only she had spoken one word, but she never dared to try.

Some girl's hearts do not possess a flame, or the flame got blown out too many times ever to catch fire again.

I wish Tricia that your frozen heart will melt the day you decide to get out of your corner, out of the coldness where he now resides, and believe me, I did not wish to be one wintry love misleading you.

Remembering the past can be positive but try not to bring it back. Leaving burning bridges behind is understandable. The important thing is not to burn bridges we still need to cross in the future.

I genuinely think that people do many terrible things for the best and with good intentions, especially if God is involved. In the end, it does matter if you do the wrong something for the right reason. Wrong is and stays wrong.

Be proud that your heart and intentions are good but be aware that we do not always have complete knowledge of the truth and good or bad.

More harm is done in today's world by people trying to do good, unaware of the unintended outcomes, or failing to do the job, than by people trying to cause harm.

For now, I will hold fast to my dreams. What would be of life if we would give up dreams because of what happened once in our past? If once I was able to feel the most profound grief, I can experience the greatest happiness.

Chapter VII

Weeks, days, hours.

The days went by during those days like flashes of light. I had been dancing with the stars. There was no person I had not excused or tried not to understand while sharing my time with Avery. I felt a universe of light raining on me. Looking back, I realize how much a person can affect your life. There is nothing like having someone holding in balance things that would otherwise most likely have destroyed you.

Clocks a device invented to warn us that everything dies, to make us understand the finality of our existence. Seconds, on the other hand, are enough to transform-limited reality into an eternity of joy.

I like and appreciate fondly about Avery because whatever we were to each other when we fell in love, we were still. I was trying to understand her point of view and to accept the differences we had. She spoke to me in the softest of tone, like she always used to do; we laughed as we always laughed at the funny little details of every single day. Most important, we were able to communicate without effort, without a shadow coming between us.

How much I longed for holding to her like this forever. One brief moment and all that could change, and nothing will be as it was before. We started a journey with no regrets to carry or pass, but we create them by the sole fact that we are humans and can make mistakes. We should lament our mistakes and learn from them, but never move forward into the future with them.

How many times someone told me, "You hurt everyone," or "You bring pain to everyone whose life you touch." I never meant to hurt anybody, but deep inside, I got used to finishing relationships in a disastrous manner.

Some actions have more significant consequences than others. But I do not have to let the result of my mistakes be the thing that defines me. I am here with the power to shape future days. With Avery, we wanted to live the life of our dreams. After all, when we start living the life of our dreams, we are building the foundations of truth, of a better reality.

During a starry night, I looked out into the sky and up deep into the stars. I beg the universe to cure me. My mistakes haunted me. If the universe is listening to me and cannot grant me my wish, I hope that the errors of my future will be new and not the old ones.

Sometimes when I spoke with Avery about my fears, I could see a slight smile coming from the left side of her lips, and that was a sign that she was listening. That is the only sure way of knowing we have someone who cares and shares our thoughts.

One day when all else fades, this moment, here, together, will always stay with me. Her presence near me, her voice will on a late evening when the rain falls, and my heart will shake still be on my mind, and I will weep for nothing.

For most of us, we remember our first kiss. The kiss that would wash away my temporary misery and let me hope again. We did not kiss during the first date nor after the second. My lips longed to kiss this girl, but my heart begged me not to it. I wanted to wait. I knew she would make me immortal with her kiss. The kind of kiss that inspires stars to shine at night and take the darkness away. I wanted to be patient, not rush anything. Some time ago, I learned that running toward something is a suppressed death wish; we crush our dreams.

The waiting may seem long, my dream of building something solid and lasting does not end. The smile upon my lips will unquestionably never vanish. As long as my eyes search for your presence, as long I am waiting here for you, there is something worth living for, something keeping me from fading.

Never will I forget our date by the lake. Not because that day we kissed for the first time. That would have been sufficient, but it is said some flowers bloom only once in a year or perhaps once in a lifetime. That day would stay graved in my memory much longer than a million years; it will see the sun go dark and the moon falling from the sky.

The night before, I had a bizarre dream. In the beginning, I was happy, lighthearted, playing in the sun, but then darkness came, and I was living a nightmare in the night of my soul. I saw myself as a demon running from feelings I did not bear to remember. My heart failed to beat, and I remembered so much and so many horrors. I was screaming when I woke up, only wishing to get out of the dream.

It was a relief to see the light of the night shining through the window. It was strange for me to have nightmares. I see now why no one ever really gets used to nightmares.

Why do we have a nightmare? Why the horrific dream that I had in my sleep? Is something warning me about a reality that awaits me when I awake?

After a while, I decided to go back to sleep. I told myself. "Dreamers constantly wake up and leave monsters behind." My sleep wasn't peaceful, though. I had the sense of rising from a world of dark, haunted places where I was alone. The only thought that brought light in those moments was Avery. I concentrated on trying to visualize her, to hear her voice, and imagining the trip we were ready to take the next day. I wanted to exile my thoughts and think positively. Slowly I felt the sleep coming back, but the sense that something terrible was coming my way did not go away.

In the morning, I forced my mind to believe that something incredible was waiting for me that day. I was tired, disgusted, disappointed with the events from last night in my head. Only when the sun came over the horizon, I felt the sunrise whisper to me the opportunity to relax and hope again.

Never ignore that anticipation is an essential part of life. I did not want to refuse the joy of expecting to have a fabulous day with Avery.

Whereas during those days of planning, the weekend had never gone quickly enough for our liking, now that we were starting the trip, we would have liked to slow time down and hold each moment in slow motion.

After we stopped to buy all the necessary groceries, we arrived at the house and did not have to go back to town. The place was spectacular, the view astonishing. The first thing we loved about that place was the scenery, and the second was to know we had all weekend ahead of us. At that moment, I was just sure I was going to kiss her. I was not going to wait anymore. At a moment when we were close to each other, I put my arms around her. I could feel her breath, our eyes met, and something delicate twinkled. She pressed me against her. It was sweet being slightly crushed by someone who loved me. The gesture of the amorous embrace seemed to fulfill all the dreams of total union with the loved one. The longing for the culmination of the waiting, a moment of affirmation, our hearts wide enough to embrace the love we felt for each other.

Avery intended to continue unpacking, but I grabbed her hand and swung her back towards me. Then I pulled her against me a second later, I felt her lips on mine, and we kissed softly, intensely, completely breathless. I have never gotten so lost in a kiss before. I opened my eyes, and her sky-blue eyes stared back into mine, and I knew I could never part from her again. I had never seen someone so beautiful as she was. I softly said, "I love your smile. I love your lips and the way you kiss me."

She looked at me and delicately said, "If we follow the beat of our heart, we will never get lost" I was the most excited I have ever been in my life. She enchanted me. I wanted her, every part of her, and I urgently craved the feeling that we both belonged there, just as we were, right that moment.

The moment was all completely soundless. I didn't think either of us was breathing. I put both of my hands around Avery's face and gently told her, "I want to kiss you until my heart beats only for you." How could I have expressed everything that came to my mind? I was only able to continue kissing her like I was giving her every kiss I wished I would have given her in the past, and every kiss I could give her in the future, an eternal kiss.

That night when we were in bed, my thoughts went back to last night. How can twenty-four little hours present you with two so different realities?

That night we did not only make love, but we also promised to make it through whatever the future might bring to us. It was more than only a pleasurable act between two people. It was a promise of hopes and dreams, of sharing life, trust, and commitment. Uniting our bodies in one was not only to satisfy us physically but to provide our soul with the power to join us eternally. To fill a void that has been there for a long time.

We laid a long time looking at each other. This girl had the most stunning blue eyes in the universe.
How could I possibly describe their beauty? She had eyes of overwhelming tenderness, warmth, and calmness; eyes reserved only for angels.

We kissed and caressed. We never realized until that moment that a single second could expand into something timeless and powerful. "You are part of me, the immortal part of my soul," she whispered to me. "Oh, my beloved Avery, I whispered back to her, "It is your love that makes me immortal; it is the intention of loving you forever."

Early next morning, she woke up before me. It was still a little dark left from the night. I remember her whispering in my ear, "Lay still, my love, it will not take me long. I want to swing before the sun comes up; wait here for me."

After the night before, it was not difficult to fall back into a deep sleep. I did not quite catch the last words. I knew it was something about her returning.

Suddenly something abruptly woke me up. I open my eyes, expecting Avery to be beside me, but the bed was empty. How much longer did I sleep? Looking at the window, I saw the light of the sun entering the house. Where is she? I jumped out of bed and went looking for her.

Leaving the house and looking at the lake, I saw Avery's body lying on the dock. Adrenaline shot into my body. I ran up to her and saw blood around her head. The moment I touched her I knew, she was dead.

There is only one kind of shock worse than the unexpected: the one for which nobody does prepare, and everybody will always refuse.

The death of the only reason for living, the approaching of emptiness surrounded by darkness asking for you, involving devouring you.

I do not remember what happened afterward, my mind was in shock, and my body shut down.

Chapter VIII

Between two worlds.

I am ideally happy. And yes, I am alone, but there was a ray of light that melted the loneliness in my heart and brought comfort to my life. Avery was in this world, she was with me, and now she is no more. There is another reality one I cannot visit, and there she stays. This place is a reality with the singularity for Avery of being able to cross into mine.

If someone had told me that there is the possibility of bringing down the Moon or darkening the sun, I would believe that, but the crossing of realities is still hard to accept even if it happened during the last four weeks each day. The result is that there is no room left in my mind for the impossible, for the unexpected. Supernatural is a dangerous and difficult word in my eyes. The idea of different realities is more acceptable. There is always going to be doubt in my mind, but I believe in knowledge and learning. I may submit to the unknown, but never to the unknowable.

I do not have to pressure my brain trying to explain the unexplainable. I could ask Avery a thousand questions, but that would deviate from why she came back to me. If she does not speak of such things, there must be an explanation. Although she is the same girl, I cannot deny that she knows something we are not aware of consciously as normal humans. For me, not long ago, everything crumbled like burnt paper in my hands, and only her love gave back hope and the desire to continue. I stopped wondering if this is all a construct of my brain. Avery told me that she does not have the body she once had. Nevertheless, if she does not have the charming smile, the deep beautiful eyes, or the golden hair, I would take her with any other form. I would take her, and I would love her again.

Then the thought crawled into my brain about the desire to touch her. If I could have touch anything in the world those days, it would have been her. There was something that did not allow us to have physical contact. She was too far for my hands to hold her but near for my heart. That was at that moment more than I ever wished for in life.

So many times, I have recreated the Saturday we spent together. There is no way I will ever forget the soft skin of her body touching mine, making love we melted together and like that day today, she lies nestled with me. We looked at the same horizons during the short time we were together, not aware that the sun was shining his last ray of light upon us.

I long to kiss her, but my lips cannot find a way back to hers. My ears and my eyes are the bridge that allows me to contact her. Happiness now is having her lips smiling at me. Why, after losing her, after having known the hurt, the sadness, the agonizing darkness of a day without her, I still long for more? I know that without being touched, I will die. The desire to kiss, touch, feel is immune to understanding the limitations imposed upon us.

Avery told me one day that for her, time was almost none existent. She was evolving in her reality. Somehow nothing stays constant. There are always changes, no matter what existence it is. Where you went last night, you cannot go today; it would not be the same place.

I close my eyes for a second, trying to get the thoughts of kissing out of my head. When I opened my eyes, Avery was in the room. She came closer and whispered something in my ear. Something about a dog called Moon or so, somewhat I did not understand. Her fingertips brushed my hand, and for a fleeting moment, it felt as she was touching me. I could not contain myself and, almost as a reflex, reached for her, but at the instant, my hand was going to touch her, she vanished. I called several times without a response. Was it so wrong to long for a touch? Did I do something wrong or destroy what we had? How was I supposed to assume that holding her was dangerous or forbidden?

Something was telling me that she would come back. It was not shocked like when I saw her dead in front of the house by the lake.

Why should I be sad? I have witnessed a miracle with my own eyes, and since then, nothing was the same. A quick thought shot through my mind. What if by loving intensely, we could give our loved one the miracle of immortality? After all, love is an essential quality in humans. An unexpected memory from Carol took me back to days long gone. To the day, she decided to end our relationship. I remember Carol telling me, "To end it now would be better than taking your dreams away." I cannot explain exactly well, but it made me feel better. I knew that Avery would never go away and let me without my dreams.

I was still fighting against the thought of losing her one more time, not wanting to give in, searching my mind for a valid explanation when something I would never have imagined happened. Someone was ringing the door. At the door was a couple, two persons I did not recognize immediately. A little hesitant, he said, "Sorry to disturb you, I did not plan to come, but my wife insisted. We are Avery's parents". I invited them in. I remember Avery telling me that her mother's name was Gitte. There was a resemblance I could not deny. After a couple of awkward minutes, I asked her if I could call her by her name. She agreed with a lovely smile. Such a smile was familiar to me; it was apparent why.

The father explained the unannounced visit and apologized, revealing the cause of their coming to GÃ¶teborg. I told me, "He had to be here for business, but at some point in the afternoon, her wife had the impulse to visit you, John." My face turned to Avery's mother and asked, "Gitte, was this impulse around four o'clock?" Both glanced into each other's eyes and, with surprise on their face, asked, "How did you know?" I wasn't ready, to tell the truth, but I didn't want to lie either. I just said, "Just a premonition, that's all."

The conversation was very agreeable. Both were kind and shared an interest in getting to know me. We did not want to speak about Avery's death, but it was inevitable. At some point, Gitte said, "Without her in my arms, I feel an emptiness in my soul that will never vanish." Paul added, "When someone you love dies, and nobody is expecting it, you do not get over it, you will never accomplish...". Gitte interrupted him and asked me, "How are you doing?".

Inside me, I wanted to tell them that she was with me every day, but I only said, "Grief is forever. It will never go away; it becomes who I am".

The evening came with unannounced surprises turning a lonely night into a remarkable one.

When it was time to say goodbye, Gitte made me promised her to celebrate Christmas at her house. At first, I tried to resist affirming that I would go, but she did not accept my excuses. At the door, we embraced and said farewell until Christmas.

Inside the house, it was quiet. All I wanted is to talk with her, to tell her about her parents. The more I thought about it, the more I understood that Avery knew better than I did about the unexpected visit. I was sure that she even arranged it to happen. Avery was the best girl I ever came across. It was unavoidable the desire to emulate her by living with the joy she did.

Even after death, Avery taught me waking up forces residing dormant in me, liberating me from pain, taking this confusion that clogged me for so long.

That night I had a strange dream. It was a good dream but confusing. I saw a giant moon, a dog, and a field full of flowers and trees. A voice was telling me, "During every age of your life, never stop dreaming. No one can take away your dreams. Life can take your possessions, your health, even your soul, but nothing can take away your dreams".

It occurs to me that the peculiarity of most of our dreams is a way of a multi conversation between our subconscious, the world, and probably also with other levels of existence. The inability to open up to other realities only blocks us from the supernatural world.

I believe now every spark returns to darkness, but from darkness, light can emerge. Avery returning to me not only stopped my heart from bleeding out, but she also opened my eyes to believe in a world more magical than I ever could imagine.

The few next days did not bring Avery back to me. Only in my dreams was I able to see her. One night I could hear her say, "You are going to feel alone. However, I am in heaven watching upon you. I am beside you now. Love is your strength and is more abundant than the total stars at night. It is time to let go!"

I had tears running down my eyes the moment I opened my eyes. Something was telling me that Avery was not coming back. Christmas was a few days away, and my mood was not suitable for the season.

When Avery died, I felt like I had lost everything, and now the feeling was coming back. I guess that anyone who has experienced an exceptional event in their life that defies scientific knowledge can comprehend the limits of human knowledge. I did not want to regret not having asked her more about life.

Something like panic struck me the day before going to Avery's parents. So little I knew about them. I missed Avery more than other days. It would have been so different; it was not long ago we discussed spending Christmas with her folk. I remember her telling me that I would have to do things for her and me responding, "I want you to be happy; I will go."

There was no chance for me to stay here and break one promise I gave her. I got in the car and left.

Chapter IX

Dark and lonely.

I t was late when I painfully opened my eyes. My head was full of misery, full of pain and dissatisfaction. I looked around, trying to recognize the place I was standing. I felt a funeral in my brain. One of the first manifestations of knowing what happened just some hours ago was the emptiness I felt inside and the wish to die. I wished not to be part of this monotonous world, which I did not love anymore. To be sent to a new one, which presumably in time I would come to hate too. Darkness is not always the same darkness. Once I was in a dark place; by the subtle randomness of destiny, I met light. That kind of light that changes you let you see things that were always there, but you had no perception of them before. The same unexplainable destiny turned that light off. Now I am still in darkness as I was but only more dark, colder, more tragic.

I did not want to talk. I was able to kill a flower just by touching it. To the world, I was dead, as dead as I could ever be. The liquor we had with Matt last night didn't push all the memories away for long.

Last night he took me to his house to keep me safe from myself. He knew that the feelings inside my head were increasingly torturing me, and in so doing, they split me apart.

Matt told me that there would be a funeral and that Avery's family was asking for me. I did not want to meet Avery's family. We talked about visiting her relatives, but I did not have sufficient time to see any of them. How could someone ask me to go and introduce myself to strangers while at the same time burying the only girl I was supposed to love? If Avery's family wished to bury her, a part of me wanted to go down into the earth with her, lay down beside her, and die with her.

Agnes, a friend of Avery, called me and told me, "It is important to attend funerals unless you do that the loved one dies for you again and again." For those words, I did not find worth in my head. What was she talking about exactly? Did she believe that? In one regard, yes, I believe in ghosts, but we create them. We search for answers to all we do not understand, including extreme cases where we haunt ourselves with our creations.

Was Agnes trying to tell me something? I did not know this girl very well. Maybe she had more contact during work hours with Avery, but Avery never said much about her. Because I did not want to be seen unconcerned with what she said, I just told her that I only wanted to survive this world that kept trying to destroy me and that I was going to think about it.

In the emptiness that was all around me, I thought of all the people coming to say the last goodbye. Every one of them was showing me a view of their broken heart. I did not wish to say that my broken heart was more important than theirs.
Although it was a great tragedy for her family, my pain was only my pain, and every one of us was feeling a different heartache. None of us willing to accept that she

was gone, some of us openly weeping over her, irreversibly, death is only a tragedy to those left behind.

After much hesitation, I went to the funeral but watched from afar. So distant that many people unable to attend, who had not even come, seemed closer to my only love final departure. The garden was full of flowers, flowers I was not able to smell.

The pastor said a few words impossible to distinguish from the distance before gently lowering the casket into the earth. All stared silently at the coffin. My tears were the only tears that I could see; I was the only one watching the last farewell from a distance like an outlaw afraid to be captured. My sad smile the only smile, wishing that this girl may find a home wherever she was going and hoping she will never forget the importance she has in my heart.

As the earth embraced her body, her soul embraced the universe. I wished she would recognize heaven with its innumerable stars and angels and never stop waiting for us to reunite.

While driving home, my pain intensified with my loneliness. Every second of the day, thoughts revealed all the things I did not want to know. The loss and the pain did not end. There was not a time when I was over missing her. I did not feel bad about feeling bad. We constantly need to endure in times of inner turmoil before the dust can settle, and we can smile again.

Between the way things used to be only a few days ago and the way they were now was a void that I could not deny. I understood my pain and welcomed it, accepted it, needed it. Otherwise, I must question if the love I felt in my heart was true. In my conception of life, I hope for a better place after this life. I am not a religious person or a believer, but I am open to accepting other options. The problem with her leaving me so early is that she took all with her: my dreams, my hopes, my future, and my reason to continue. My life was full of her light now, I had entered a lonely, sad, and empty world where I knew missing her would never get easier.

A soul can live in torment for years and years only to be released from the pain by death. Deep inside, I knew she would have wanted me to be happy again. Without thinking, I knelt in the grass of the garden, fighting not to give up and at the same time admitting that her departure broke me. I would never be free of Avery. Like a flower that once has blown and knows now must forever die. I do not want the pain to bring me down; I must fight, I must do it for her, but the sensation of cold and darkness was everywhere. Like a cold rush, the memory of the nightmare returned, screaming to me, "It was a warning; why did not you listen?" I was scared. If everything in my world turned black, how would guilt affect me? If it is heavy, you cannot fight it. It just takes over and stays with you ruining you to the point of turning you into a shadow of the man you were. I did not why, but I got up, looked at the sky, and screamed, "Do not go, return, please return to me."

Was I going to be haunted night and day by nightmares, monsters, and demons I did not even believe? No! I was going to love her even if she would never be beside me for the rest of my life. Avery, I love you every day. And now I will miss you every day.

The second night after her departure, only mourning accompanied by whiskey and the sound of the rain was with me. I ignorantly searched for a way to escape reality. For some reason, suffering men always hope for comfort at the bottom of a bottle, perhaps consciously aware of the devastating result. When ordinary life chains me, I had to escape one way or another. Obviously, I could not continue for long to exist sanely under conditions of absolute misery. All were allowed that night; maybe temporarily whiskey could help, but never completely.

I told myself, "Remember that grief is a necessary pain." I had a long night ahead of me, fueled by the force of a thousand regrets.

Chapter X

Darker and days.

I choked back tears today when someone from the police came to give information about the accident results. The officer was kind and worried about not hurting open wounds in me. He told the investigation concluded that Avery injured herself jumping into the lake and, while trying to reach the house, collapsed and died. Most probably, she did not see well in the still darkness of the morning and hit a rock with her head. A terrible accident, he said and gave me his condolences. I brought him to the door and thanked him. He looked at me and said, "A good heart has stopped beating, but I am sure she will continue to live in yours." Then he turned away and left.

Everyone gets trapped by disastrous times that fall unexpectedly upon them. I was and did not want to be the exception.

Only a few days after her departure from this world, everything around me was meaningless. There was a silence in the house that let me hear how my heart was breaking. It was a slight, clean sound; it was like the sound of crystal glass breaking.

People from the office called me intending to help, but I wanted to be alone. I knew these wounds would never truly heal, and they will continue to bleed again at the slightest word mentioning her name or, what is worse, at the mentioning of any other girl's name.

I needed to look at my life. What I saw was not pleasant. I had one serious love relationship in my life, and it had ended in tragedy.

I was a mess right then. I was not able to sleep, and I did not want to be awake. I threw myself on my face on the sofa, and with my heart in fragments, every sensation was more vivid, every pain stronger, regretting things an average person would never recognize. I do not know where I was at that moment. It was not in this world; I was also not somewhere else. Only the sound of something smashing in the kitchen brought me back. What was that? What could have fallen? There was no way someone could be in the apartment. I got up and went fast to find the origin of the smashing noise, constantly trying to find the explanation. I walked into the kitchen expecting something, and it was nothing. It is harder to find nothing when I knew of the opposite. How was that possible? So many thoughts rushed through my mind. Did I imagine the sound of something breaking? It was the only plausible answer but not a convincing one.

Maybe I needed to relax and make sure that my mind would not start to play tricks on me. I went to the bedroom and lay down in bed. There lying with my arms crossed behind my head, glared at the ceiling, wondering, trying to understand what just happened.

The memory of an afternoon returned to me. Avery walked into my office and said while we were working, "You seemed so far away from my office I had to check on you." I smiled and said, "Oh, I was. I was swimming with you in the deepest ocean, far away from land." Avery replied, "It is wonderful. I enjoy swimming". Happiness is part of who she was.

We both knew nothing is permanently perfect. But there are perfect moments, and we believed in those moments. We were invariably aware of our luck and entirely decided to bring about more perfect moments.

She was the girl who confused me with an angel when she looked into my eyes, not knowing it was the reflection of herself that she saw. For me, she was the perfect girl, good-looking, sweet, and smart. The perfect balance of danger and charm, utterly attractive almost in a forbidden way.

The bitter knowledge that we could have had something perfect brought tears again to my eyes. Why was it not meant to be?

Those were the times I thought I was going to die any minute, and those were also the times when I was afraid the pain was not going to stop, not even after death.

It must surely be a tribute to people's resilience in love that some men and women who lost everything and arc walking through hell survive the pain.

I got up from the bed. I needed something to distract me from myself. Looking out of the window at the boat in the river made me wanted to go for a walk.

The sun was setting, and it was chilly. Walking through empty streets was good. Hardened by the recognition of my truth, I became cold and genuinely indifferent. Nothing mattered much. How many tears were necessary? One day my crying was going to stop; my tears would dry up and run out. That day I would stop being human and transform myself into a monster unwilling to share more tears or feel anything again.

Oh God, what's wrong with me? The thing about living alone is that it gives you a lot of time to think. But thinking is not what I wanted. It was in the sleep of death that I saw my only escape. I longed only for the darkness, and in the dark streets, I was willing to stay for hours, for days, maybe even for years, trying in vain to find comfort in life without her. I saw only an empty world around me.

The thought of dying was stronger with every step I took. A peaceful death is praiseworthy. The source of anguish lies not in leaving life but in having lost that which gives it meaning.

I was a man walking through the night before extinction, with full knowledge that the sun was going to shine again but devoted to wishing desperately that the night would end with me too.

The street ahead of me was bright with lights. I looked up the tower before me, lifeless, concrete and glass giants stretching for the sky, reaching toward the darkened sky. Could it be the solution to all my suffering? Just a few days ago, I woke up from a nightmare; I was relieved. If I only knew then what I know now. I woke up only to wake up into a nightmare.

Could I get up to the very top of the building? Getting inside was easy. There were a couple of restaurants and bars open.

My best choice seemed to go to the hotel and the bar. If I could get a room on a high enough floor, the rest would be more straightforward. Their terror of falling from a great height was still alive in me, but with the help of alcohol, I hoped to find the strength.

After having some drinks, the fear of falling remained changeless. The alternative here was the other terror, a life alone. All was dark, sad, and empty falling to death became the slightly less terrible of two horrors.

At the bar, I saw a flyer with information about the swimming pool on the 24th floor. It was like the universe showed me how to find the peace I was longing for during the last days.

Did I want to die? I wanted to believe that no one jumps from a building because they want to die. Most people kill themselves because they do not see a way out of their misery, guilt, or want to stop the pain.

Something was pulling me to get up there to the pool. The view was unusual, extraordinary, and contradictory to my state of mind. I never heard of this place, and nobody had mentioned it to me before that dark night.

My heart started to pump faster. The awareness of ending all through the ultimate decision was avoiding me to feel the effect of alcohol.

Some time ago I went to bed and had a terrible nightmare. A few days ago, I woke up into a nightmare. I planned to end the pain. I would die any minute soon; that was not scary; I was afraid to jump and not die. I felt an urge not to exist, something I have never felt before.
Everything affects everything we do. Because it was late, only a few people were still sitting there; it was a perfect deserted area.

The moment of choosing the last thoughts was now. I had never understood love, and when I did, love took me to heaven and threw me to hell. The truth is love did evade me until the very last. Carol and, most powerfully, Avery gave me a glimpse of the meaning of love. The closeness to her rose me to the sky; the absence showed the abyss and drew us apart. The final rapture was her passing to the other side. A departure not announced, not expected, not deserved but mortal. Now my life was fading; I was alone, ready to embrace death.

I claimed a protection fence when I heard her call my name. The unexpected call, the shock of listening to her voice paralyzed me. I looked around; there was nobody in sight.

Tears run from my eyes. It was as though she was trying to save me from going to hell. My lips were suddenly trembling. Did she know? In my mind was only the awareness that Avery was my last chance to be happy, that I loved her and had lost her, that she would never return.

Was I losing my mind? No matter what universe brought me there at the age of a cliff, another was saving me.

Fighting with unknown mysteries and alcohol in my veins is how I got through many a dark night like that.

Chapter X1

Illusions.

It is so odd how we can believe in dreams, but we wake up, and everything collapses. It is far harder to face reality after dreaming of heaven. In my dreams, I have Avery with me.

One day everything will be well. That was my hope but that morning, getting out of bed was arduous, to face reality even harder. I wished to continue dreaming until I become a dream myself.

Though the room was quiet, something in the atmosphere had shifted. I sensed the presence of somebody in the apartment. I knew that someone could not be there. Then again, the sound of something breaking. The sound frightened me beyond anything I had felt before, and it was the third time the same sound. I went to the kitchen, and there she was, Avery. I saw her face and stumbled back a step. My heart raced. The image of the spirit, whatever it was, waiting there for me made my heart pound out of my chest. She looked at me and said, "I cannot begin to explain to you this." With a smile, she added, "I am a ghost. I am not here, not really. What you see is the image you have of me. I have not a body but felt your pain; I had to be with you." At that moment, I wanted to get closer, but she told me, "Careful, John," Avery warned. "Don't get too close. We cannot touch."

I was on the verge of going insane, desperate mad; these are symptoms of my brain not willing to accept what was right before my eyes. I asked, "How is this possible? Are you OK?" But, at the same time, I knew that letting this get inside my head was dangerous.

Avery was so vivid, so real. Very softly, she whispered, "Do not be afraid, I am good I must go, but time is not what it used to be there. I could not lose you else like that, without even the chance to say goodbye". After a pause added, "I think dying was a little out of my control."

My mind was not able to grasp, to understand, to believe anything. Avery was trying to connect, and I refused to allow my mind to accept. I could not let myself admit it if I wanted to survive. The risk was too significant and my anxiety too strong. I sought to turn and run away, but that would have crushed me. How could I? In her eyes, I could see the sadness that reminded her ghost of the body she had left behind. Avery, is it you? I asked her.

She said, "I am not the same, I have not my old body, here the laws of physics do not apply the same. There is not only your imagination, but my essence is also composed out of matter. Different from all you know. We cannot interact as we used to, though I will stay until you can let me go".

Suddenly, in place of Avery was an older version of her. John, she said in a lowered tone, "This is me at the age of 60". "I will always use the form I had while with you but remember, nothing is as expected. You are still in the realm of life, but now you have already an impression of the realm of the afterlife".

After those words, she dissipated into nothing, and I found myself not knowing or remembering how I got back in my bed. When I opened my eyes, it was already dark outside. It was as I did not dream at all. My memories came back, and only at that moment, thoughts of her returned to me. I did not know where I went or if I did anything in the lost hours of that day.

Ghost is representative of the usual West Germanic word for "supernatural being." Skepticism of being sane is a most grievous burden, and to wake up with highly confusing sentiments does not make it easier. All the mourning feelings seemed somehow out of place. On the other hand, she was officially dead and would not come back to life.

Why do I get the feeling that this does not have a happy ending? Something was terribly wrong or was I close-minded, and this was the most beautiful gift I could ever have dreamed of? Is it possible to love a woman who does not have a heartbeat?

Is it not strange? I have spent most of my life trying to convince myself that I am not a lost cause. That in me still existed something worth finding, and now in these bizarre circumstances, all my beliefs about reality are crumbling down. I always believed that doing right did not invariably mean that you did so. Could it mean that honest loving is much more extraordinary than we dared to dream?

I was not sure this was a world I belonged in anymore. For me, God is a human creation. It does not mean I do not accept the possibility of a God. It means that I do not believe in any of the Gods presented to me so far. If what I experienced is not a trick played by my brain to escape the emptiness Avery left behind, then something does exist after death, and alone that thought changes all my interpretation of life.

As the hours went by, I wanted to see her again. Maybe talking to her would open my eyes a bit wider. It was inevitable this wanting to be with her, but somehow it didn't seem right to wish to see her. Suddenly, the music player started playing a song we liked called "We are never apart." I knew she would be there. I walked to the living room, but this time my eyes expected to see her. Although my heart was beating faster, I was not troubled. With Avery, we spend our young love visualizing the existence we thought was waiting for us on the other side of our illusions. I do not regret anything we did. It is good to dream, to imagine, and construct a future in our heads, but we should not forget to enjoy each moment as it happens without destroying that enjoyment.

I could not believe how right I was. Avery was precisely there where I imagined she would be. She lifted her eyes the moment I walked in and smiled, saying, "The quality of a man is in his assumptions," as if she knew or could read my mind. I smiled at that, and then my gaze shifted to a spot beside the sofa where she was sitting. There was the book that I had lost weeks ago and that I could not find again.

Only she could be, so concern to feel such love without knowing it; she did not seem to be different from the way she was. I was astonished, and before I was ready to speak, she looked at the book and said, "I am like obedient dogs and will come when I am called, including bringing things your poor human left in a backpack you do no longer use."

It was another of those rare moments when I did not know what to say or do. If for a moment I thought I was accepting the fact of Avery being here, a simple action was utterly messing up my head. I chewed on my bottom lip for a moment and told her, "Sweetheart, have patience with me; you have shaken my life in too many beautiful ways. I will need you to understand". Avery's smile shifted, becoming sweeter, lighter as if she could see much deeper into me. She did not hesitate long before answering, "Love, I am just not clouded as I was before, that is all" With almost no voice, and with a raspy sound, I just told her, "Thank you."

We went talking for hours with no stop. Every minute with Avery, my heart was healing from all the hurt, pain, and darkness of the past days. I wanted to keep looking at her, at her fascinating eyes, at her face and lips, which I would have given anything to kiss.

Suddenly, she tapped a finger against her right temple and said, "I need to let you rest, let me go. Remember, I am not saying goodbye; I only want to kiss you good night."

It always took me a considerable time to return to this reality. I took the book Avery left on the table of Deborah Leblanc, opened it, and read from it. "But you know, mon petite, what you got is a gift. And when the good Lord gives you a gift, you have to use it. That's why he put you here on this earth..." I could not continue reading. It was like everything was telling me that it was OK, that I should not be afraid or perturbed.

I glanced at my nonexistent watch, went to the kitchen to check the time on the microwave, and could not believe it. We spent almost four hours talking without pause. Time is nonexistent when I am with her. It may be plausible that we got lost in time, and how could this affect my functionality in this world?

The next day was going to be my first day back to the office after the death of Avery. I could not pretend nothing had happened, and I was also not going to play the role of a devastated lover who lost the love of his life.

There is not a single chance for me talking about Avery coming back if I did not want to end in a maniac house. Part of me was accepting the madness that could be explained by saying that my response to reality was to go insane.

I have found both peace and refuge in my insanity. Maybe I lived in a unique world, a secret world different from those populated and experienced by other humans. It was not a new world; on the contrary, it is the same old world but with a unique new set of truths.

Was I ever crazy before meeting my eternal love? Maybe. Or life is simply crazy. For now, I would act as I lived in another dimension, and I did not need to destroy my happiness even if crazy is my new name.

Many people were trying to avoid having contact with me. Some were eager to make me feel better, and some just ignored me altogether. Actually, the problem is that I cannot blame anybody. I would not know how I would have dealt with such a situation, so I did not take it personally.

Mark being my closest friend, had given me plenty of space, always helping me with the social responsibilities I so unwillingly was ready to handle.

We had a long conversation while having lunch, and he said to be very surprised to see me taking all so well. It was hard to look him in the eyes and not to start crying or laughing. If I only could tell him the reason why my face was quiet and my heart not frozen.

I watch him return to work with glittering eyes, knowing that he was a good friend but uncertain to be ready for my madness. Other people came to express good wishes, but I was in shock at some people's words. More often than not, we are not careful or cautious of what we say until we see that the words we selected did hurt the other person's feelings. Many well-intended comments cause the opposite of our expectations.

Regardless of all, the first day went well until I saw Avery coming my way. I closed my door and did not know what else to do. She walked into the office without opening the door. She looked at me and said, "I am the happiest creature in the world. Sorry, that may not be inventive; perhaps other people have said so before, but not one was me". Not knowing what to say, asked, "I suppose the question must be, are you good"? She laughed and replied, "Love, do not be scared; we are safe, you are safe." Before she finished the words, Matt walked inside without knocking, I almost faded. He explained something, not aware that Avery was only a few feet away. I thought to myself, now the world will end, but to my surprise, Matt kept on talking as all was normal. After a brief silence, he looked and me and asked for my opinion. Sometimes, a chance must be taken to improvise an answer, but I was going in the entirely wrong direction this time. Matt's face was accordingly astounded. To my relief, Avery told me what to say, and with a nervous laugh, I was able to fix the mess. Matt, laughing, went out and closed the door behind him.

Staring at me," Avery said, "They will not see me, John, only you are capable of seeing me." I asked, "Do you have a plan?" Looking strange, she said, "A plan? What plan? I'm making this up as we go."

I sat down and said, "I am sorry, sweetheart, I am still new at this." Usually, she always kept a certain distance from me, but that morning she came much closer. Only a few feet separated us. It was as she could whisper something and I could hear the words coming from her mouth.

I got up, but she took a few steps back. She said, "Someone is coming soon but remember that settles it, no more being afraid of other people when I am with you, OK?" Avery was smiling, and I was convinced.

One other girl from the office commented after the meeting later in the afternoon that it was nice to see me smile again. I was not aware of that, I told her but thank you for noticing. I wanted to say to her, "There is a thin line that separates laughter and pain, and now I have reasons to laugh again," but I kept the thought to myself.

Tonight, I wanted to talk with my reason to smile, with the girl I love, with the girl who loves me even after death.

Chapter XII

Christmas eve.

We should live as we dream. It is the only place where we never lie. The truth was that I would much rather have stayed home. The days were hollow and my home empty, but I did not have the desire to go anyway. Days were passing by, and I was only staking days in my life without much significance. I miss her, and I miss the ghost of her. Avery was the drug of energy I needed in my life to spin me out of the miserable monotony of present days.

Yes, the promise I made forced me to get in the car. Luckily the traffic was light, and I was on time as I arrived at the house. There was no moon. Although the weather forecast announced snow for the night, the air was not cold. The sky above my head was pitch black but looking at the horizon; it was still some light in the distance. It was almost four o'clock when I rang the doorbell.

Gitte opened the door and welcomed me. There is no better hospitality like when someone tries to understand you. She knew it felt hard for me to come and accordingly wanted to make me feel at home, something I appreciated dearly. She was the first person to smile at me that day, the first in mentioning that Avery would have enjoyed sharing the night with us.

Gitte introduced Lone, Avery's older sister, and Charlotte, the youngest of the three girls in the family. She must have been 25 because, according to my knowledge, she was two years younger than Avery. Paul came to meet me and took me to the living room. There I saw a fox terrier, and without realizing it, I called him, "Moony come, come here." Everybody looked amazed, I would say, everybody was stunned. Lone asked me, "How could you know the name?"

Charlotte added, "It is impossible; how did you know?" I realized that I needed to explain it to myself first, but then I remembered the dream I had with Avery, and I understood. The problem was now to find a way to explain it more credibly to her family. The truth seemed the best way to go, so I related my dream. Fortunately, everybody, besides being surprised, did not give it more thoughts.

I caught sight of myself reflected in the window of the room, and for a second, I saw Avery at my side. I wanted to call her, to see her again, to talk with her again. The saddest outcome of our love story was that probably I would end up missing her longer than I loved her on earth.

Paul gave me a glass and said, "It is a pleasure to see you with us." Charlotte whirled, turning toward Lone, her eyes wild and blue like Avery's. It was a relaxed atmosphere surrounding the room; it was easy to feel at home.

Lone asked, "Do you like Swedish girls?" When I did finally speak, I surprised myself by saying what was on my mind. I was honest; I said, "Never in my life, I thought I would meet an angel, but it happened, and she was Swedish." Gitte took a glass and said, "SkÃ¥l Avery, in your name, my baby girl." with a sad but proud voice. It was a short silence after, but the air was untroubled and calm.

As it is a tradition in Sweden, Gitte and Paul had prepared the traditional "Julebord," a rich table with a delicate and tasty variety of meals.

I was happy to have decided to come. We are never too old or too young to receive healing waves of a family, especially if in a way it was my family too, or more precisely it could, it should have been.

Christmas waves a magic wand over this world; it is a shame we do not celebrate it more often. It was called the Holiday Season in the old days, but I think it is not a season rather more a state of mind. It has little to do with the original meaning; nevertheless, it brings harmony between many.

Talking with Charlotte, she told me that she would study in Göteborg for a few months. She was very excited about the change coming in her life. She was planning to use Avery's apartment. The rental contract was valid for another eight months, and to her, it had a sentimental value.

Later that evening, Lone left the house to hang out with her boyfriend and left the four of us to enjoy the evening.

The hours we spent, they had merely the eï¬€ect of a miracle. In so many forms, they changed the way I perceived the world, the entire universe. Moments like these made me aware that the more you reduce your viewport of life, the smaller your world becomes.

It was not life's fault that my days were so similar that I kept sliding into memories or trying to see the ghost of Avery as my only option to be happy.

I was sure that Avery wanted me to be here. While enjoying the evening, all my troubles have started blurring together, releasing new hope and pleasure of being alive.

As I was relatively far from home, Gitte had invited me to stay overnight. We had time to talk. While chatting with Avery's parents and with Charlotte, I felt as I knew them forever. I was feeling each of them with my heart. This feeling came to show me that connections are made with the heart, not with language.

Charlotte had many traits of Avery. Of course, that would not have surprised anybody, but I felt a sort of tender curiosity. I wanted to keep talking to her so that I would know her better. A connection can only be cultivated between two people when both bring something to make it possible. Something inexplicable in her nature spontaneously revived strong feelings in me, and I was ashamed of myself. I was sitting with Gitte, Paul, and Charlotte, the closest people to my deceased love. How could I ever let feelings toward her sister grow?

Gitte asked, "Are you glad you came?". I said, "Delighted, I did not know it would be so nice to be here. Thank you". Paul added, "We wanted you to be here, thank you for coming."

The willingness to surrender to ideas when the evidence is against better judgment is highly dangerous. It was the type of displays of affection, either verbal or not, that most impacted me. It was something natural in the way Avery's family acted that I had never expected.

I could not have been more wretchedly blind before coming. I was here, and I started to care, started to feel attachment, and there lies where danger spreads. Caring was a thing with claws. The more I felt attracted, the deeper my claws were ready to claim a victim.

It was getting late, but we kept laughing and talking. When people laugh together and are having a good time, they tend to talk and touch more. Eye contact happens more frequently, attraction manifests, and all was chaos inside me. The beauty and mystery of this world only emerge through moments like these.

The sort of tender curiosity I felt before turned into a lot of interest. If I add my natural foolishness, the result mixed with the wine we were drinking resulted in uncontrollable appetite.

Charlotte exchanged more prolonged eye contact with me while her smile got sweeter and sweeter. She was so delicate, so soft. I have found it isn't easy to remain sitting and not get closer to her. Her eyes were summoning me to get nearer, and the logic in me was drowning with every sip of wine. All my defenses turned against me, overrun by her voice calling surrender.

At one point, Paul stood up and said, "Children, please stay up a little longer, but I must go to sleep." Gitte followed him and, before retiring to her dormitory, said with a smile on her face that denoted honest words, "Do not stay too long but stay a bit longer. We need to get some sleep". We wished good night, and they left.

Sitting there with Charlotte was like standing on the brim of the volcano, waiting for an eruption to occur. I intended to keep distance and avoid the nearest of her, although I secretly craved for it. I wanted to know what makes this girl smile, what makes her cry. There was nothing I did not want to know about her. Assuredly, whomsoever put me here had intended this to happen.

I had to control my foolish heart and go to sleep too, I told myself. I said to Charlotte, "It has been the most wonderful evening in a long time. I think we should also say goodnight." She replied, "Are you tired?" To which I said, "Not tired, enchanted." Charlotte looked at me, touched my hand, and sweetly said, "Then stay with me a little longer." It was the lightest of touches but made my skin burn.

And that feeling, that feeling of being accepted, was all over me. Whatever new doubtful thought I had in my mind respect Charlotte's affection dissolved with a word of her mouth. Receiving love and appreciation is the only key to get out of pain and doubt, of misery.

I looked at her and said, "I think you are going to drag me to hell and force me to stay there" She laughed. "I will try not to take it personally," she said. Then she said, "You are an idiot, one I seem to like." I whispered in her ear, "that it was the most precise thing ever a girl has called me; I am not only an idiot but a mad one."

I touch her cheek, holding her mouth on mine, so I could feel every place where our lips touch and softly kiss her. It was a delicate, tender kiss we did not want to stop. After a silence, "Are you okay?" Charlotte asked. I wrapped my arms around her. "Listen, my heart is beating again," I said.

She looked into my eyes and intended to say something, but instead, she gave me a light rain of butterfly kisses. Outside I was the same person; however, inside, I was never going to return to be the person I used to be.

Since she has been the kisser and not the kissed, I wanted to return the light rain of butterfly kisses with a kiss to remember and said lovingly, "This kiss, my kiss, is a kiss that will steal your heart, may I kiss you?" Charlotte did not answer but closed her eyes and tenderly got closer. It was a sweet burning kiss, one that stole breaths, stopped hearts, and left a mark nobody could ever erase.

Chapter XIII

The morning after.

Even though my brain was a mess, the morning was welcome. For the first time in a long time, my heart was buzzing, making tenderness out of agony. The thought of seeing Charlotte was enough to make me smile, to make the whole world bright and new.

It was a tendency of me to be so preoccupied with what her family would have to say. In order not to lose support and care before we went to sleep that night, we decided not to show our newly found attraction until the right moment openly. Anyhow, we would be living in the same city, which would give us plenty of freedom to meet and build our love.

There is no better occasion to demonstrate a genuine determination of affection than the ability to remain quietly together without awakening suspicious. We both knew that the news of our love would come as a shock considering how little we knew each other and the nonetheless fresh death of Avery.

A house is never empty with a pet in the house. Considering that everybody would get up a little later on that morning, I offered to take the dog for a stroll. As I was leaving the house, Charlotte came running to accompany us.

I was savoring the pleasure it had given me to hear her coming. She immediately said, "You did not think I was going to let you go alone, did you?" I reduced the space between us and kissed her forehead, then said, "I could not risk someone seeing us. The trees have eyes." She sputtered with light laughter, saying, "And what could they have possibly witnessed that would have looked suspicious?" Well, I said, "A boy, a girl, and a dog." She smiled.

Accordingly, to the weather forecast, it had snowed last night, not much but some. It was cold, and the wind lifted her hair. Like her sister, she had long golden hair. How beautiful it was to watch her hair ruffled by the wind, eyes crinkled against the sun, and an everlasting smile. We did not care about the cold. We ran against the wind blowing in our faces, laughing and talking.

Back at the house, breakfast was ready. Lone was the first at the table. I could see something in her eyes how she looked at us when we walked into the house. That was when it was all made painfully clear to me. She would not see with good eyes our relation. I do not think Charlotte noticed it; she was the liveliest, happiest person I had ever met.

Maybe I was a prisoner, Captive of my belief and love when I arrived at this house. Now before leaving, I was free of the chains nobody, but myself put on my arms, legs, and heart. My conscious was troubled, but I did not think for a second that Avery was not the architect of those days.

I was sitting with her parents when I saw Lone and Charlotte coming to join us. Charlotte was staring at me from a distance. I felt that I would do anything to have that look cast upon me for the rest of my life. There is undoubtedly a peculiar grace, both in the gleaming eyes of a loved one as well in the eyes of someone saying goodbye for the last time. It is the happiness and the sadness shouting joy and pain.

Like last night the conversation was cordial. The most superficial exchange of ideas was entertaining. Also, like last night, after having spent a short time with us, Lone stood up and said, "Sorry guys, but I have places to go and things to do.' Her father asked, "What do you have to do?" Lone shook her head, saying, "Father, you know. I told you days ago that I was having lunch with Markus." She unexpectedly hugged me and said farewell. I told her to visit me, to what she only said, "Great, who knows" and went away.

Out of respect for me, everyone mainly spoke English, but I wished I could have used their language.

If I could by magic speak Swedish with all the complexity and nuances of the language, I would surely be pleased.

We continued the dialogue, and for me, it was a mystery how we could engage in such an exciting conversation. We were being fascinated with nothing at all but exchanging opinions. Charlotte's father was an engaging personality. He was spontaneously adding witty comments that kept the conversation entertaining.

Later at the table, Paul was talking about his experiences while visiting America. He was very astonished by the appetite for loneliness people have over there. He believed that the same helped people to be more open to talk about personal issues. Some stranger can tell you about his or her divorce, their job, or the latest lover affair. Europeans, on the other hand, are more reluctant to open their life to strangers.

I think every person is a unique world, although some characteristics must apply to all societies.

After lunch, when we were alone, I told her, "Your mother was reticent during lunch." "Do you think she can feel something?" asked Charlotte. Precisely at that moment, Gitte walked in and said, "It's a dangerous assumption, and I know I should not jump to conclusions, but is something you want to tell me?"

Charlotte and I looked at each other with guilty eyes but did not know what to say. The reaction of Charlotte was lovely, proper of an angel. She stood up and embraced her mother; I understood something but not everything she said softly in her ear. The mother thanked her and, without more words, left the room.

Charlotte then came closer and put her arms around me, saying. "Yes, John. All is good. Just one thing, please believe in me. I do not fall in love so easily, but with you, I did". I had to kiss her before saying, "You touched me, and I was yours. Your voice touches all of me, trust me when I say this was meant to be."

From that day on, Gitte was never the same to me; something inside her was blocking the sweetness I felt yesterday.

Slowly it was time for me to return. Charlotte reached my hand; I grabbed hers. I smiled and leaned forward impulsively to kiss her. She was smiling, but tears were rolling fresh on her face. She was not ready to say goodbye. Charlotte, the love in your eyes, the pain you took from me, and everything else you gave me is all I am now. Two weeks will rush by like raindrops in a storm. Do not speak of goodbyes, do not mention distance because, in your heart, I stay.

I dry her tears, but new drops were ready to fall. She said, "But now it hurts to watch you leave so soon." Why do goodbyes always create a crack in our hearts? Could we not just smile at an upcoming Hello?

Charlotte informed her parents that I was ready to leave. Paul was the first to say goodbye. Gitte was polite and friendly, but her eyes hid words she wanted to express or maybe did not how. I left the house; only Charlotte accompanied me to my car. We knew that we could not kiss. So, I just got in the car and drove away without not even whispering goodbye.

After one mile, I searched for excuses to turn around and have one more chance to hold her in my arms again. I thought I was tougher than the word goodbye, but sadly, the most painful goodbyes are the ones that are left unsaid, believing or hoping the pain will not come.

Driving home, I was joyously returning by her side with my thoughts. I wanted to use the phone and call her, but we agree that only she would contact me.

Yes, I was jealous of anyone waking beside her, jealous of the wind touching her face, jealous even of the moon and the sun that could shine on her while I was alone.

Before going home, I drove to the house by the lake. I did not talk appropriately to Avery, and I was going to do it now. After some hours I was there. Since the day I tried to touch her, she was missing, not from my mind but absent from my eyes. I never liked to call her a ghost, but the word reflects the state of not being on the same reality level.

I knew she was not going to be there, but in a way, I was doing this also for myself. I went to the shore of the lake and stood there in silence. There was a pale moon. Clouds came and went hiding the fading light of the night. I hoped she was still able to hear my voice or read my mind. Avery, I came tonight to thank you for the greatest gift of love you gave me. I sincerely believe that you did not want to leave me alone. The love I felt for you and you for me made the impossible possible. Today I am not sure of what was real or all tricks of my mind, but that doubt does not make my time with you less eternal. In my heart, it was real and always will be. I will never say goodbye to you. You will never say goodbye to me, and there is no doubt about that. Thank you, Avery. I love you always and forever.

Once at home, where the memories of Avery haunted me most, I felt at peace. I was open to seeing her again, never afraid of what she could say. I knew that night I was falling asleep with hopes and dreams that I rarely had since Avery left.

The night was silent. The missing of her voice was getting louder. When finally the phone rang my heart was screaming for her. The sweetest voice on the other side said, "I'm dreaming of you, my eyes are crying. I'm missing you". I told her, "Never cry; we are never apart." We continued talking until late that night. When we said goodnight, it was very late, but the minutes or hours did not matter; we were together. Every time I open

WhatsApp, the first thing I did was to check whether she was online. It did well to know even if we did not text.

It is lovely to have the technology to keep you connected, but something gets lost in words, which is hard to explain in the language of symbols; it is the touch of her skin, the taste of her lips, the sparkle in her eyes.

Chapter XIV

Göteborg.

Being home was thoroughly different this time. I still remember closing the door with a cloudy mind; I wanted to stay here, not spend Christmas with people I did not know well. I was being pushed around by the uneasiness in my mind of not having Avery near me anymore. I had to step outside my comfort zone to keep a promise I made.

Confirming that the most challenging times often lead to the most significant moments of your life is out of the question. Today all is back to the happy days I had with Avery. I should be grateful to her for every second of happiness coming my way.

I never liked to call her a ghost. It sounds cold, impersonal, almost scary. Avery was better described by the word Supernatural. Supernatural is a word for anything that does not fit our present knowledge of the elements of this world that are somehow inexplicable.

I took a shower, had a snack, and relaxed on the bed listening to music and remembering the voice of Avery that was still present in the room. When the phone rang, the voice of another angel said, "love, are you home already? I miss you too much, you know?" Listening to her speak made my chest hurt for a second; I wanted her to be here. I did not want to miss her. "Nothing can feel the emptiness of you here, my love," I said to her. We continued talking for a long time. Neither of us wanted to say goodnight.

Before hanging the phone, she sweetly said, "It is painful, loving someone from afar." I do not how many times during our conversation I told her how happy she was making me. It is simply not enough to say it once. Finally, I said, "Charlotte, you make every day mean something. Know that wherever you are, I will be thinking of you. Sleep, tight love."

Around me were the echoing voices of two girls changing my life with immeasurable force. Avery was with me not a long time, measured by a calendar but left a mark more profound than any other person I ever knew. I cannot explain, I do not know if she was physically here or only on my mind, but she was real.

I have been asking myself so many times, "What if Avery was the answer?" Not because I do not believe but because I am not sure myself of what I saw. It is controversial; it is not impossible to think there is more to our reality than meets the eye. I will not share my experience with anybody, not even with Charlotte. Not until I can be sure that it was not my mind playing tricks on me that created her ghost. What good would do to confuse her?

The house was quiet as always. Night air approached, and I needed to get some sleep before starting a new chapter, this time together with Charlotte. I felt fortunate to have love in my present. I thought of Avery but not the same way my thoughts entangled me with Charlotte. Avery was a love that was from another world. She did prepare the road for me to find her sister, and confusing as it may sound, I accepted. Would someone understand me?

Charlotte never said a word of feeling guilty or regretting us being together.

At work, everyone was as if the world would not change. All aspects related to work were so material-oriented that sentiments are not existent, completely disregarded, and not part of the world.

During lunch, I had to speak with Matt and tell him about my newfound love. He listened and, in the end, said, "There are two possibilities, and both do scare me. The first is you are lucky, or you have a mess up heart".

After my convoluted love experiences, the opinion of a friend was vital to me. Sometimes an outsider can see better the road you are following. If someone had told me to give up my relationship, I would never take the advice, no matter the cost, but would pay attention to my loved one to see if she could get hurt with my love. If I do not bring a smile to her face, then I must let her go.

My phone was ringing. Incredible, how much does the ringing of a telephone excite my heart. I took a deep breath and answer. Charlotte was in a good mood, unwilling to breathe while talking. She was out of herself and said, "John, I will see you this week. I got the confirmation from the university today." I could not believe this was real; she was telling me I would not be alone anymore. I said, "Let me wrap my arms around and kiss you. Please hurry to me." After that, I only heard her say, "Yes, yes, my love," and the call was over.

I squashed the little voice of doubt about doing the right thing, looked to the horizon, to the setting sun, and said, "Charlotte, I do not love you out of loneliness or unhappiness. I love you because you are you."

The rest of the day, I was longing for another call so bad that it began to hurt to care so much. At home, I ordered something to eat and waited.

I want to take back at least half of the "I love you's" because only lately the meaning is clear to me. I did not care anymore that years had gone up in smoke. The future was bright, and I was ready. It took longer than expected, but suddenly the vibration of the phone accelerated my beating heart. "Hi love, I have been desperately waiting for you to call me," I said. She started laughing and reply, "Sorry, I know, but I was not alone, and I wanted to be so that we can talk with no disturbance." She added, "Do not you think that we are out of our minds?" I agreed, saying, "Yes, love, we must have caught the same disease." The minutes went by, and our phone batteries must have run out together. Charlotte promised to call again tomorrow. Before hanging told me in her sweet voice, "I want you in ways that I know you would find shocking," and she was gone, not giving me the chance of saying goodbye. It was the second time our conversation ended that way.

A time ago, part of me realized that I was a monster.

Carol was the first to open my eyes and show me how wrong it was to play with other people's hearts. A time ago, I was looking to end my life, tired of the hurt in my heart, and Avery saved me from hell. Today, Charlotte was lighting my world, shining the light of love upon me. Girl, I need too much of you. A lifetime of nights spent at your side would not be enough to satisfy the thirst for you.

The next day at work, it was hard not to deviate from thinking about Charlotte. During working hours, it was not surprising if I did not get a call. She knew that it was not always easy to talk, but later at home, the phone did not ring. Only late in the night, I got a voice message.

The voice of the message denoted some sadness, "John, it is a disaster to miss you. I made the mistake of telling Lone about us. She disapproved and, what is worse, told my mother my confession. I feel so betrayed. Now, you can understand that the air unbreathable in the house. I am so sorry, I should never have told her, but my heart wanted to shout it out loud. I will call you tomorrow, sweet dreams, my love."

I took a deep breath. It did not come as a surprise; not everyone would understand our relationship. I was having thoughts about what other people could say. Lone undoubtedly had reasons that Charlotte and I did not share but valid in her eyes. You cannot feel betrayed by someone you do not trust. It breaks your heart and leaves scars not easy to forget. Nobody can go through the pain and not feel forever cut in the heart by the hand of betray.

The moment after reading the message, I wanted to call her. To tell her everything will be OK. But I know it is easy to say, not easy to accomplish. My call would also be the drop that could ignite a more terrific fire. It hurts not to be by her side when she needs me most.

She was going to call me, and I did not want to miss her call. At lunchtime, she called. Her voice was not as always, something worried her, and she did not hide it. Charlotte said, "I am so depressed. Not because of my sister but of the decision of my family not accepting my choice." I needed to comfort her but did not how. "Is there something I can do," I asked her? She answered, "I appeared to be oblivious to the surrounding reality. I want to run away. To leave all behind and go my way alone."

Those were strong words I could not ignore. The responsibility of changing the lives of her was waging hard in my head. I did not know what to say, but she could misunderstand my silence. I did not want that to happen. I told her, "Charlotte, you have me. If you decide to go your way, I am unconditionally here for you." I heard her sobbing and said, "Would you take me? I may not be the angel you think." I only said, "Always, my darling, always." After a silence, she said, "Wait for me, I will call you again, I love you." and again she was gone with no goodbye.

I knew people that spent years together and never ended knowing each other; others may need only a day. I wanted to believe for us a day was all we needed.

That night she did not call me. That day it was Saturday; consequently, I did not have to go to work. Dawn through the window woke me. I looked outside; the weather was fine abnormal, sunny for a January day. I checked my mobile phone, and there were two messages. One was from Charlotte. I read it, not knowing what to expect. She wrote, "John, it was not easy to decide what to do, but I am coming to Göteborg today. I want to see you. Please do not feel obliged to do something you do not wish to. Love Charlotte." I typed back, "Sweet loved Charlotte, as soon as you leave the house, call me so that I can call you. I am waiting to see you."

Around noon the phone rang. I picked up; Charlotte's voice was clear, more relaxed than the day before. I did not want to talk only about the things hurting her, do not like dwelling on that, so I asked, "At what time are you arriving?" She said, "At four at the main train station are you going to wait for me?" Laughing, I responded, "I am already waiting for you." She only said, "Good, I love you," and was gone.

Before the arrival time, I was at the station. It felt surreal to be waiting for Charlotte. Carol taught me that without trust, love could never exist. You should not expect trust; trust is part of love; if you do not have it, you do not have love.

What was our next step? I asked myself this question a thousand times that day. I was also confident that what we were looking for will happen.

The train arrived, and people started to descend from the train. I looked in the crowd, and I saw her, then focused directly on her until she was in front of me. We briefly kissed. I said, "With you next to me, I am whole again. I miss you. I feel lonely when I can't see you." She smiled and said, "I am where I wanted to be."

Later at home, she explained in detail her two last terrible days. It was the first time she ran from home. She could never wash the taste of trusting and being betrayed from her lips. It would take time to cure the scars; they were too fresh to heal with words. It was necessary to look ahead, and the miracle of being together was the best beginning we could have imagined. She said while helping me to fix something to eat, "No one will see the marks burned In my heart. No one will know. But they will be there."

Later before going to sleep, she asked shyly, "Did my sister ever sleep with you here? I smiled and said, "No, she did not." She never mentioned that again, but I guess it made her feel less weird to know.

Because she came to Göteborg without the blessing of her parents, she could not use the apartment of Avery. I told her that we were home here and that she should not worry about being herself. We agreed to take our life together slowly with no pressure on either of us.

We went to bed, accepting not to rush into love. We wanted to savor every step in our relationship.

Every instant was as we had no choice but to rejoice in being close. We caressed, kissed, and entangle our bodies, not knowing if the world outside us still turned or existed.

The easiness of communicating our desires overpowered our resolutions and better judgment. The longing for each other was just a part of us, and we ended making love, not knowing how to avoid it.

Chapter XV

Not alone.

L ast night before falling to sleep, I was afraid to close my eyes, fearful that I would open my eyes the following day and find myself alone again.

We fear things because we value them. It was better than heaven to wake up and see Charlotte still sleeping at my side. I started to seek the right words to tell her how she made me feel. I am constantly trying to express what is in my heart which could only be possible if she was me. Words will never rightfully be able to convey our feelings.

No one ever told me that dreams felt so real. Lately, I have come to face experiences I could not discern if they were true or fantasies. Lying next to this girl was one of the fantasies I wanted to keep forever. There is a sort of invisible sheet between the world and me, and it is hard to know on which side to stay.

If I value the present means, I fear losing it. All the desire to change the way I interacted with women created the fear of not loving. So, the fearful past causes a frightening present.

Carol would have told me, "I cannot have a man who is afraid of everything," and probably she would be right. Fear is not so difficult to understand, but we should not let the unknown dictate our course.

I wanted to wake her up, but I could not bring myself to do it. She was sleeping so peacefully. What would we do today? What plans do we have?

None of these questions needed an answer right away; besides, we do not always need a plan. Sometimes we should take the time to enjoy the moment; we need to breathe and see what happens.

I have been dwelling between contrast. Life threw me up, almost scratching the stars, and fell into abysses from which it was practically inconceivable to return. I was determined to hold to Charlotte and to go far beyond the visible stars. An exceedingly warm vision of the future was illuminating my future.

Softly I embraced and kissed her cheeks. We stood there, not moving, nearly not breathing, just enjoying each other.

I asked, "Does it hurt? To wake up." "Silly you," she said and added, "It takes some time for me to wake up, get used to me, love."

"What would you do today, have breakfast, go for a walk to the park, go shopping, or conversations in candlelit at night? "All the previous, all of them," was the answer.

Breakfast was the first and the easiest to fix. I am usually not too fond of breakfast in bed, but this was a memorable day with extraordinary rules.

We had so much to talk about, and being lazy for a day was not relevant; the consequences were miles and miles away.

We took a shower to refresh our bodies but returned to bed to decide what we would do the rest of the day. We did not fix our thoughts in planning the day; we scheduled an eternity and included other ideas in case we ran out of time.

At lunchtime, and a little ashamed of ourselves, we ordered pizza and continued the conversation. Our plans were not ready yet.

Between planning, we included a lot of kissing. We had to set the rules and sealed one by one with a kiss. We wanted to risk everything for a future worth having.

Charlotte was finishing her studies and would attend a semester at the University of Göteborg. She smiling asked me if I was happy to be together with a psychology student. I remember telling her, "My love, if you are a fish, I will be your water."

We cannot let work distance us. This world is not simple, and it is not easy to get lost in decisions. We must listen to each other; we need to speak without words, talk without sound, and follow the same dreams.

Dreams should light our path; following our dreams will define us, and our love will make it possible.

There have been times I have thought love was only a game played to satisfying basic instincts inherited since the beginning of human history. Charlotte is the other side of that thought, and I would hate to find myself thinking not similarly as her again.

Only watching Charlotte's lips took my attention away from the words coming out of her mouth. I had to ask her to repeat the question. "I love you," she murmured. She knew I was crazy for her. For a moment, she looked at me; she did not say anything, and only after considering her words she said, "John, I would not mind staying here forever entwined to you." She tried to speak, but my mouth was over hers again. She tasted sweet, like honey; I do not remember breathing as we kissed, our tongues playing together until we had bruises on our lips.

We tear into each other as if we wanted to be one. Under the sheets, the language of desire, the hope of belonging, and the dream of never part took every hour of the day, returning the notion of completeness.

We had intimacy, connection, feeling, youth, time; most important; we had us.

Everything was happening so fast. It was as we wanted to love ourselves for the lost time we spent away from each other. The day we met, we connected, and words ceased to exist.

A twinge of uncertainty induced her to ask, "Did you not promised conversations in candlelit at night?" She was right. It was dark outside; we did not get out of bed since last night. We went to the kitchen, studying possible ingredients to prepare something to eat.

It took not long. Our dinner was ready. While Charlotte finished the freshly prepared meal, I lightened up the candles for the long-promised dinner.

This evening was time for us. Nothing outside mattered to us. We had turned our phones last night and were not planning to turn them on again until tomorrow. For this reason, even the pain caused by the sad events of the past did not exist. There are a million reasons to not selfish, but we needed one day to only think of ourselves; we needed to find the way to be one. Inside each of us is a deep craving for happiness for belonging. It is essential to be selfish, to be honest before being there for the world. If you do not know yourself, what can you be for others?

Without honesty, we can build nothing at all. It may not be easy to believe, but that day she shaped me, and I chained her to my side for the rest of her life.

Charlotte gave me the strength I did not know I had. During the coming days, our relationship was going to grow deeper. The day spent in bed was never going to fade away from our hearts, no matter how distant we could grow in the future.

While I was doing the dishes, Charlotte went outside. On the brick terrace, she stood looking up at the stars wondering in silence. Only a day ago, she was living with her family. My arrival in her life changed her world of that I was well aware. I plan to consume all the time necessary to make her happy; I wish never to let her down.

There was a slight breeze that night, a cold breeze enough to make her shiver. She came with a freezing face back inside the house. I had to embrace her to make her feel warm. It feels good to care for someone, especially I longed to have a heart beating beside mine.

Before closing our eyes, I said to her, "Give yourself to me. I will always be there for you, I promise." With closed eyes, she murmured, "I already did; I am yours eternally. I am your girl."

When you ask a woman, "Are you, my girl?" And if the answer is vague, then, you know. Hesitation is a reflection of a heart in doubt. Do not blame the woman. She is honest. You cannot tell someone to love you. You can only wait until she does or says goodbye.

That night she fell asleep before me in my arms. I wanted to watch her sleep. Her breathing was relaxed, her face an inspiration for my dreams. She was the only real thing in the world. With my lips touching her forehand, I fell asleep.

Chapter XVI

Timeless and clouds.

I t does not take me long to get out of bed. That morning it was different. Seeing Charlotte sleeping beside me was painful to leave her side. Trying not to wake her up, I went to take a shower and ready to go to work.

When I returned, she was still asleep. One advantage of the winter is the long nights. I kissed her head softly and left to go to work.

Shortly after eight, I got a call from her. She said, "Why did you not wake me up? I wanted to say good morning." With a half-smile, I said, "I did not want to disturb your sleep. There is a copy of the house key for you on the table. I miss you, call me later."

She told me that after talking to me, she wanted to call her parents. It does not matter how disappointed she was, but her family was a fundamental part of her.

People in the office may not have noticed, but I was not the same man that started working here a time ago. Nobody could know how many women there were in me. Without them and their effect on my life, I would be half the man I was.

Work is a way of expressing who I am, and I seldom do not enjoy being at work, and hardly ever my concentration let me down. That morning my thoughts were with

Charlotte, going back to her constantly, reviving each of the minutes of the last day. My head was chaos in poetry. For the first time in ages, I did not stop glancing at the clock on my wrist, waiting for the end of morning work.

During a short coffee break, I call her and told her to come and have lunch with me. She gladly accepted. Knowing she would come soon calmed my foolish heart, and I could concentrate on my work.

How could I be able to forget those eyes, that face? If she was not there, at least, she was firmly in my heart.

At one o'clock, the front desk called me, announcing that Charlotte was waiting for me down in the hall. It did not take me a minute to get down to where she was waiting for me. Nothing kept me rushing to her and kissing her lips. I said, "Thank God you are here. I missed you too much." Her face was sparkling, and her eyes showed her love the way only honest love has the right to shine.

She was not happy to tell me that the conversation with her parents did not go well. It did not go wrong but was cold. She said with a somehow broken voice, "I do not want to talk about it; it is not my intention to bother you with it." I disagreed with her. Holding her hands, I said, "Why do you not want to speak out your life miseries?" Adding, "For, after all, you do not know what they could be doing inside your soul. Share the good and the bad; I want all of you." She kissed me and said, "Sorry, you are right."

The time had passed much too quickly. I had to return to work but not without first promising to be home early.

An awake heart is like a lighthouse helping others to find a safe way home. Your actions are more compassionate; you are more willing to stick your hand out and support others; it simply makes you a better person.

With Charlotte coming into my life, things that mattered to me before ceased to have the same meaning, where I live, where I work, all of these I would give up to be with her.

Me talking to myself said, "I would not survive if she dies." At the second my words came out of my mouth Avery came into my mind. I felt a sudden sadness; now seemed like a million years away from our time together. Thinking of her was not bringing pain anymore. Deep inside me, I knew she took all of my pain and left me with the happiness of Charlotte. Carol showed me the meaning of love, Tricia taught me the danger of a frozen heart, but Avery showed me what love was and saved me from hell. I would never betray Avery consciously hurting Charlotte.

While driving home, Charlotte called me, saying that she was at the grocery store not far from our house. I should meet her there. That Monday afternoon, it was snowing copiously, but I could see her waiting at the entrance. We kissed hello and went inside the building. She wanted to cook and needed diverse ingredients that I never used. Everything was entertaining with her, even shopping.

At home, we unpacked the bags and divided the fun. I went to take a shower, and she started preparing the mysterious meal. She said to me some days after, "I've never known anyone who likes to shower so much." There was not much to say besides agreeing and laughing.

Back from the shower, I embrace her, kissed her, and offered my help. She prepared a family recipe widespread in Sweden, "Meatballs & Mashed Potatoes, Cream Sauce and Loganberries." The best-known recipe is the concept of "Mom's Meatballs," which, of course, are supposed to be homemade.

We had a great time. It was better than going out to any restaurant in town. It did not matter how often we were facing each other I could not take my eyes out of my sweetheart. She was happy to see me enjoy being at her side. During dinner, she said, "This is our purpose: to make the rest of our lives as meaningful as possible, to enjoy every day as the last." The connectedness between us was born from the very first time we met. It was hard to believe that she was a stranger in my life only days ago and now my only sunshine.

Like last night and many more coming, she enjoyed walking outside the house after eating, and I was in charge of doing the kitchen work. Something I did not mind at all doing.

The little snowflakes floated down on her eyelashes and covered the head and shoulders. I could not stop laughing when she walked inside. She was disguised in snow. I felt the cold that flowers must feel when the snow gently rest on them. And like last night, I embraced her to make her feel warm again.

We were happy. And this is true of much of reality but what we think of as inherent properties of the world are merely effects of multiple causes coinciding.

During the following days, Charlotte started going to the university. On weekends, we explored nearby cities or tested the many options this beautiful city had to offer.

When spring arrived, we were planning to travel abroad for a few days. There were so many things we wanted to see. So many places we wanted to go.

"I would love to see your hometown," said Charlotte quietly one evening, her gaze absent and distracted.

After two years away from home, the idea of going back did not sound bad. We agree to spend next summer in America.

It was spring, but we still had many days when it snowed. Usually, while visiting the countryside, we went for long walks. There was just something beautiful about walking on snow that nobody else has walked on. Strolling through the forest was something we enjoyed much. We had the feeling of being home in nature. It was our paradise being together hand in hand in the yellowish winter twilight across the snowy places. How white the sun that enters this forest making everything shine.

Charlotte was my ray of sunlight, turning the cold of the landscape into a summer day. One would have said this woman who wore a gown of winter frost blinded my eyes. Helplessness has weakened me, but her love strengthens me more than ever before.

By the end of May, we wished for the return of sunny days. I recall one morning when Charlotte opened the curtains, exclaiming, "Oh, no. I was expecting a kiss of sunlight and got slapped by rain."

That may have been the most significant difference in us. I was an Autumn person, and she was definitely a summer girl mixed with attraction to snow.

Unconsciously, I tried to forget one of those beautiful days. Not because of anything Charlotte said or did but because of something I saw, and she did not. As so many times before, we were walking in the snow when something caught my attention. In front of me, I saw footsteps, two pairs walking, heading to the sunset, but after a few steps, each went separate ways. That was odd, and I commented this to Charlotte. I said, "Is it not strange, the footsteps over there?" She looked around and quietly asked, "Where, darling?" I pointed to the footsteps, but she did not see anything. The footsteps were too obvious not for her to see them, so I did not insist and instead changed our conversation.

Some time ago, I had a terrifying nightmare. That night, I could not return smoothly back to sleep. In the morning, my conscious me did pretend to find reasons not to let the nightmare affect my reality. Soon after that, I lost Avery, and I blamed myself for not listening to what the universe warned me.

After that day, my mind as been trying to find an explanation. Trying to blame the reflection of light, the shadows, imagination, or anything else for what I saw.

I started to be more protective of her. First, she was happy, but she began to feel suffocated by my worries with the passing of days.

As I well recall, that was our first argument between us. I searched for the slightest way not to sound out of my mind, but it was impossible to explain the nightmares, visions, and ghosts to someone without creating a void full of doubts and worries. If I had told her about her dead sister talking to me or that somehow, I could see things that were not there, she would have begun to mistrust all of me, and I was unwilling to let that happen.

The only solution was to ask her for forgiveness and to promise to refrain from being so controlling.

I told her, "Sorry, my love, please try to understand that the fear of losing you blinded me." She gently smiled and said to me, "Do not think that I am not afraid of losing you. You are my world." We ended our first argument with those words, but I felt the hollowness in my soul and that the world was darkening on me.

Chapter XVII

Sun rain and storms.

You wake up on a summer morning feeling happy and pull up the curtains, and what you see is only a shadow of yesterday. Our dreams are one of the most fragile things disappearing from our minds almost as soon as we open our eyes.

Day after day, I have been fighting not to let my fears destroy my happiness with Charlotte.

Today we had reasons to celebrate. Charlotte was getting her Ph.D. in psychology and, from that day on, starting her professional life.

The girl of my dreams was still trying to wake up. Slowly she came to the window where I was and opened it. A rush of warm late June air invaded the room. It was going to be a hot summer day, the perfect weather for a deserved celebration. I stuck my head out to see if I could see any clouds approaching, but nothing was in sight. I took a deep breath charging my lungs with air, and returned with her to bed. We knew how the celebration would best start.

After breakfast, I drove her to the university and continue to my work. The plan was to meet later. I kissed her goodbye, not knowing that a quick goodbye would be our last kiss on this world.

Arriving at my desk, I gazed out of the window to one of the first cloudless days of the summer. Maybe it is wrong when we remember specific dates as the beginning of a chapter in our lives as it would not be something occurring due to many extraordinary moments.

Shortly before noon, I felt a sudden hurt in my head and my nose started bleeding. I took a handkerchief and held it at my nose. At looked at the clock; it was precisely 11:53.

I remember calling a meeting off and driving home. Nobody needed to say something I knew. I felt it with no doubt that Charlotte had an accident. My phone rang, a voice informed me that Charlotte was in the hospital that a car hit her and I needed to get there.

Arriving at the hospital, a nurse asked me to wait and informed me that a doctor would soon speak with me.

This time nothing was a shock like before in my life. The inevitable was less a shock. I could tell by the way the doctor was walking the news I was going to receive. I knew everything before a word came out of his mouth. Why should my existence repeat itself, again and again? I asked myself without giving much attention to what the doctor was saying. The only words I remember to hear were, "I am very sorry."

That afternoon I took a flight back to America. I asked Matt to take care of all my belongings and gave him a POA to do all necessary. A POA is a document that allows a person to appoint somebody to manage your property, financial, or medical affairs for you.

I never again heard of Charlotte's family, at least not of the family residing in this world. There was nothing to forgive; there was nothing to change anymore.

I started helplessly to believe I would always be at a point where I no longer had a chance to be happy for an extended period. The day Avery died was the most profound horror I had witnessed, but now I just accepted her departure, regretting not having loved her enough to change her destiny.

The idea that loss gets easier with time ultimately proved wrong when Avery died. There was no point in establishing the possibility to be different from Charlotte. There are too many stars in the sky, and for me, it was enough to know how far the first was from where I was.

Even though it may look like the devilish side of me was gaining ground at the end, it may show that I did not care anymore what sort of person I would end being. From now on, I did not want anybody to share my life. As long as I live alone, I would be safe from hurt, pain, and suffering. Happiness did not matter in my existence anymore.

Understand something universe, I will be hated by many for not caring for my human fellows, but my heart broke too many times and in too many pieces to hope for better days. If I ended living on the streets one day and somebody looked at my face should know that appearances are not always correct. Probably no one would see the pain and grief of losing my two angels in less than a year reflected upon my face.

Dreams cut by the grief of losing love wither and dry faster than the ashes of heart drying in the hottest desert. The problem with love is not that it does not return or breaks your heart; it dies. And when it does, you die too never to return.

The devil comes untouched by feelings to steal, kill and destroy, but he happens to look my way; he probably turns around and cries.

Money was not going to be the main factor in my short future awaiting me. I rented a cheap room in a small city on the west coast. During the nights, I walked the streets and visited every open bar willing to sell cheap whiskey. If I could find my way back, the days were there to sleep and rest my weary head.

My smell helped me to keep people far enough not to get starting a conversation. My life was as empty as my heart.

On Saturday, while sleeping in the park after a long night and many drinks, a police car disturbed my peaceful sleep. I knew it would happen at some time, so I was careful to always have all the required information they could legally demand. There is no law mandating you to smell or dress according to some dress code, so I was free to continue my new lifestyle.

It was great. I was having fun. Night in and night out after having seven beers with a couple of scotches, all was confused enough, and trying to think seemed an impossible task during those nights. Days were too short, and mostly I spent the early hours finding a place to sleep if I did not remember how to get to my room.

I was drinking a little too much, a little too cheap, and try a little too hard trying to continue, never stopping. Often managing to get home to a cold bed and thinking, "That was fine. One less day to go".

Waking up, my first thought was, "I will drain that glass again. I will keep my demons drowned in whiskey." No monster was able to get near enough to mention names capable of touching my soul."

It was a mixture of complete oblivion of myself and perfect disguise that left me unable not know the face's name looking back at me when staring at the mirror.

Alcohol did not manage to ruin me financially. Morally, I was over the rules writing by people and physically did not matter to me. It was a question of time until freedom was granted to me. More alcohol I was able to consume less, I was able to see its effect on me. There was never a chance to fight the demons of the past because no monster survived enough the influence of whiskey. Music seemed unknown, and the only piece of sound worth hearing those days was the sound of alcohol filling my glass.

The stains left on my soul could be seen only in the sunlight, so I avoided the light of the sun more and more. During the daytime, I slept, and only the night was my company.

What is this thing people call substance abuse? It does not exist on the contrary. Life is abusive, cruel, and merciless. I seek to never remember, forget the hurt, the pain, and most of all, the illusion of love.

Hollow and empty are terrible ways to feel when once you were close to light and dreams. The only way to not let memories return was to place all energy in blocking any flame of yesterday's shine on the present.

I was good at keeping memories so deep inside the abyss I was dwelling that slowly I did not even remember my name. The person I used to be, was nowhere to be found. The words that once could have broken any intention of escaping lost their meaning. I was able to walk during daylight without remembering why I hid. The nights were not an escape anymore, only darkness and emptiness.

One day waking up, my desire for whiskey was gone.

I was free of the torture of hell. I had crossed hell, and now my body demanded sleep needed to rest. I didn't understand why there was sudden relief as if I woke up from the worst nightmare that lasted a million nights.

I took a shower for the first time in months. The water running down my body was taking the smell of hundred nights away. I wanted to get out. I went outside, bought new clothes, and walked like a zombie through the streets of the city.

Everything was new to my eyes. I entered a coffee shop and asked for a sandwich and juice. I looked at my hands and did not see them trembling. All was new to me. My name slowly returned, and with my name also memories of yesterday. I could feel my life and my pain returning. Every memory was coming back. I revived angels that will not fly by my side anymore. Returning outside, I looked up high into the sky and cried.

The sound of an old lady brought me back. She was standing in front of me and said, "Sweetheart, I am telling you, stop running, stop hiding. If you loved someone the way you suffered, you love them the only way, your best way, and no time would be enough for you to forget without forgetting yourself. Does not matter if you had a hundred years," she told me. "It would not be enough."

Chapter XVIII

August.

One day in August, I fell in the water during a walk beside the sea; instead of getting out, I started swimming into the ocean, not looking back, not worrying about losing strength. I kept swimming until the water was above beside and not only under me. I did not feel pain or desperation, only a floating feeling of non-existing.

The sun in my eyes woke me up. Where was I? My only memory was me swimming running away from everything. I should be dead or mad. The desire to try again crossed my mind, but I felt just an inner indecisiveness telling me there was another way.

Right now, the shadows of my thoughts were dragging me back to the city. Walking the streets was not helping me to understand. There was nothing there but strangers doing whatever they always did, nothing which connected me to them.

Back in my room, I cleaned all the garbage and empty bottles that laid around. I wanted to get some food, but my feet were tired my body needed more rest.

It was getting dark when I woke up. I had a good sleep without dreams. My mind more relaxed there was no thought rushing to perplex me of being alive. There was nothing more beautiful than the easiness with which the sun refuses to stop shining. The sea was dragging him down, but the sun kept shining even under the water.

Before going to sleep, I wanted to get some food, so I make my way to the grocery store. I went inside walked through the corridors, searching for something to buy, but my appetite was gone. I had not even desired to drink anything.

The night was calm, and only a smooth breath from the sea touched my face.

I really do not know why I always loved the nearest to water so much. In a sophisticated manner, we are committed to the sea; it brings the notion of our beginnings a billion years ago. The impulse of going to swim took control of me; I had to get in the water. Many hours later, I was still swimming. Nothing made me feel tired; more time I spent inside, less I wanted to get out. There was an ocean of silence between myself and the rest of the world.

There was nothing wrong with watching the cost from far inside the sea. It was beautiful, it was endless, it made me feel as if I had the moon, the stars inside myself. I was the ocean, and the shore was part of nothing and all. Peace was everywhere.

Walking again by the beach, the sun rose far on the horizon. Although I spend all night swimming, I was not tired. After some minutes, my body felt light, almost like floating, and I closed my eyes to relax.

Again, like yesterday, I woke up without any memories of having dreamt anything. It was again sleeping without dreams. Walking toward the pier, and remembered how

Avery loved to hang over the edge and watch the sun go down. She loved it, especially when the waves were high, and we could appreciate the power of nature talking to us. There was a magic about the sea we both shared. The day was cloudy. The sun cannot hide like the moon but produces beautiful shadows while passing over them.

Charlotte said to me once, "The ocean makes me feel tiny, and I am grateful for that." The memories about Avery and Charlotte did not bring pain nor the fear of tears getting in my eyes. Every moment I was more at peace with the world that not long ago shook my life with ups and downs, burning my heart with passionate love and breaking it mercilessly.

I kept strolling down the coast; somehow, it was not necessary to return anywhere. Nor did I want to ask myself questions that only would confuse me. I was feeling uncontaminated from the problems of the world for the longest time I remembered. My strolls grew longer each day. I had no direction, no place to reach, only a romantic wish to kiss who lived in my heart.

One day I left the path across the coastal line, and my feet walked toward an old memory. I turned around to watch the ocean one more time. Somewhere inside me existed the desire to one day be part of that ocean. The new path to that summit I so much longed for took me to a place I could recognize no matter how many moons had passed. The house by the lake was the same nothing had changed. I was not aware that until that moment, my heart never had beaten; it had been silent nonexistent, only coming here revived it. Inside the house was Charlotte.

Waiting outside was Avery. Her eyes shining the light of thousand stars. Her smile the smile of thousand angels.

She took one step to get closer to me and said, "I have been waiting for you, love," and extended her hand towards me. For a split second, I remembered the last time I tried to touch her, and she had vanished since then. Softly I reach for her hand, but now I was able to feel her. It was not a touch of two skins longing for contact. I felt entangling myself with her, connecting like the night we made love. That night I was trying to get tighter than our bodies were allowing us. With every movement, I was getting closer, not only more intimate, but I was melting into one with her so that I started to be her, and she was me. When I looked at Charlotte, I did not know if I was Avery or my old me.

Charlotte was coming my/our way; she had tears in her eyes, tears of joy. Softly as before, we got slowly closer until we were all one and the same spirit.

We had given the final kiss of our worldly existence, and now finally, we were completed. We left the house, left all memories of earth behind, and started to walk hand in hand into the horizon.

A long time ago, I wondered why Charlotte ended our phone conversation abruptly; I never asked her, but now without asking, I knew she never wanted to say goodbye, not even on the phone. We were now like one drop of rain that once were divided in three. Each drop found a way to entangle with the other. Falling to the ocean together is our dream, to be the ocean our last destiny.

Zeitfracht Medien GmbH
Ferdinand-Jühlke-Straße 7
99095 Erfurt, Deutschland
produktsicherheit@kolibri360.de